THE DO-OVER

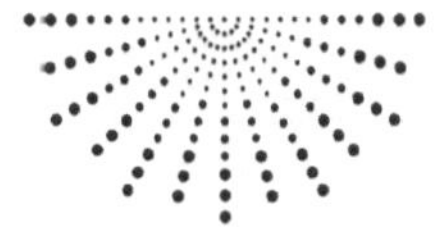

PIPER RAYNE

Cover Photo: Wander Aguiar Photography

Cover Design: By Hang Le

1st Line Editor: Joy Editing

2nd Line Editor: My Brother's Editor

Proofreader: Shawna Gavas, Behind The Writer

About The Do-Over

She was always the one.
Or so I thought.
Turns out my instincts were dead wrong.

Years ago I was faced with the choice between two women.
Both were perfect in opposite ways. One was carefree and
against commitment. The other was a woman you'd bring
home to mom.

I was young, naïve and stupid. I'm sure you can guess who I
chose.

Now, I'm older, wiser and know what the hell I want.

So, when the same two women pop back into my life it's my
chance for a do-over. But they flipped the script. Just like me,
they want different things now. Leaving me with one choice
—convince the woman I want that she wants me too.

THE DO OVER

CHAPTER ONE

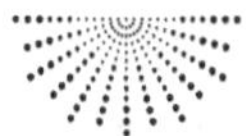

Knox

"How come female police officers don't get all the googly eyes you men do?" Patrice takes her sandwich from the pick-up counter and glances at a table full of women checking me out.

I don't have nearly the same ego as my friends, but I can't deny that I'm a good-looking guy. I also have twenty-twenty vision and I can see all the wedding rings on those women's fingers as they sip their coffees. It doesn't take police training to figure out that they're at this all-night sandwich shop because of the crying woman in the middle. She hasn't glanced in my direction once.

"It's the whole fantasy thing. They imagine me using my cuffs on them while I worship their bodies."

We find a two-person table by the windows and sit, quieting our radios so as not to disrupt the other patrons, but leaving them loud enough that we'll hear a call come in.

"I don't think they're thinking anything like that when it comes to Ben," she deadpans.

"Leave Ben out of this."

She opens her sandwich. "Ben needs to get off desk duty and run a mile or two."

Ben was hurt a year and a half ago and just never got off desk duty. He's fine now and his injury was a result of slipping on a piece of garbage but he insists he prefers paperwork over policing now. It's a running joke at the station. One of many.

I straighten the paper from my sandwich and pick up half of my Rueben.

"I should have gotten the Rueben," Patrice says before nibbling on her turkey club.

"Then get the Rueben tomorrow." I bite my sandwich, ignoring her stares of longing.

She lifts the top of her bun. "Ugh, they put mayonnaise on it. Didn't you hear me say no mayonnaise?" She moves to get up from the table.

I sigh and push my sandwich toward her.

"You're the best partner a girl could have." Patrice smiles wide and bites into my Rueben.

I grab the corner of the paper her sandwich is on and lift the bread, seeing no mayonnaise at all. She laughs then chokes on her sandwich, quickly grabbing her drink.

I point at her. "That's some insta-karma right there."

Switching sandwiches isn't really a big deal. She's been my partner for three years, and she's got my back whether we're dealing with a busted window or a bank robbery. Not that our small town of Cliffton Heights sees a lot of bank robberies. Over the years, I've debated heading into New York City where there's more crime, but then I'd have to leave my friends. And when you grow up in a shitty neighborhood where your friends are the ones you depend on when you're out of the house, you view them as family. Dylan and Jax were foster kids and hung out so much at my house, they're like brothers. We ran the streets and got into some trouble but I always knew they had my back.

Hopefully with the detective position opening up next week after Louie retires, I'll see some bigger cases. I passed up the opportunity to apply for promotion two years ago when I was dating Leilani because she's not exactly police officer wife material and I cared more for her than I did my job. But like my mom always says, looking in the rearview mirror never did anyone any good. I have to stop thinking about the time wasted and take my shot now.

Our radios squawk on our shoulders, and Patrice's hand raises to answer the call. Sounds like it's time for us to go. I pick up Patrice's original sandwich and toss it in the trash. She carefully folds the paper over the Rueben and shoves it into the bag for later.

Great, she's going to eat in the car again. I hate when people eat in the car and she knows it. Half the reason I took her sandwich was because by the time we waited for a new sandwich, she'd have no choice but to eat it in the car.

She smiles at me, lifting her bag like a taunt.

"What's the call?" I ask, waving to the shop owner before opening the door for Patrice and exiting the small deli.

The table full of women all giggle like thirteen-year-olds, watching us leave.

"Looking for someone." She opens her door and I get into the driver's seat.

In the years we've been partners, we've come to agreeable terms. One of those being we share the driving even though, and don't tell her, I'm the better driver. I won't even mention the time she rear-ended an armored truck we were supposed to be guarding. She'd just tell you about the time I hit a pothole so fast the tire flew off.

Our sixty-five-year-old dispatcher Mildred's voice comes through our radios. "Suspects shot paintballs at male and female as they left Cliffton Heights Country Club. Victims believe it to be an attack on the female's fur coat, but they hit the male in his groin. He's being transported to the hospital. Suspects' descriptions are two males in their late twenties. Not any more to go on than that. And a female in her twenties with long dark hair in a ponytail, believed to be Hispanic."

I drive us in the direction of the country club, looking for the suspects.

Six hours later, we've pulled over a few cars, responded to a domestic abuse call, and kicked kids who should've been home in bed out of the riverfront area. We stroll around our assigned area, still on the lookout for the suspects of the paintball incident, but no luck. At this point, they're probably long gone, on the highway back to New York City.

Rumors around the district are that it was the Floyds who got shot with the paintballs. The Floyds are the wealthiest people in our city and tend to have their name listed with top billing at every fundraiser. Another set of partners took their statement at the hospital, and besides having a swollen set on him, Mr. Floyd will be fine in a few days.

"So? Gone on any dates lately?"

I groan that Patrice has chosen to bring up this topic now. She's happily married, and ever since she said, "I do," she thinks it's her part-time job to play matchmaker, though she says her friends are off-limits.

"No."

"Please don't tell me you're still fucking girls and not asking for phone numbers afterward?"

I turn slowly down a dark alley. "Why are you so concerned about my love life? Other than the fact that you're in marital bliss and seem to think everyone wants what you have."

She's quiet for a moment, which for Patrice is unusual, so I arm myself with a few comebacks. "You're too good of a guy to just be the douchebag who disappoints women all the time."

"Did you just call me a good guy?" Rarely do I receive compliments from Patrice. We have one of those relationships where telling one another what a dumbass the other is being is our way of showing love.

"You know what I mean."

I shrug. "Maybe I'm still getting over her."

She blows out an annoyed breath, not having to ask who *her* is. "Give me a break. She's a felon."

"A few protest arrests doesn't make you a felon." And there I go, sticking up for the woman who broke my heart as if it was a twig underfoot—with no care for its fragility and no backward glance. Still, I'm over Leilani now. But I don't want a relationship, and if I say I'm over her, Patrice will make it her personal mission to give me heart eyes for someone.

I slow down as we near my apartment. My buddy's shop, Ink Envy, and his girl's bakeshop, Sweet Infusion, are right here. Rian is usually already baking at this godforsaken hour, but it's the dark-haired girl walking down the street who grabs my attention. I know the cadence of that walk. I know that ass.

What the hell is she doing here?

Patrice looks at me when I stop the car, then follows my line of sight. "Fits the description of the female suspect, right?"

I hold up my hand, put the car into park, and quietly shut my door. "Leilani," I say into the cool morning air.

It wouldn't be the first time a witness has labeled

someone with olive skin as being Hispanic rather than Polynesian.

She's in jeans and a sweatshirt. Patrice is wrong—Leilani can't be one of the suspects. But on her right jean leg, I spot paint, and the more my eyes scour her clothes, I spot the cast of spray on her clothes.

"Knox." Her voice is as sweet as candy as she saunters to me, her hips swaying, her eyes eating me up as though she's going to welcome me with a kiss after she bolted from town. "It's been so long."

I nod. "Since you left me, you mean?"

A door chime rings behind me. Although I don't bother looking, I know it's Rian.

"I came back to see you. I was going to ring the buzzer, but I didn't want to wake you." She breaks the distance between us.

I grab her wrist to stop her before she touches me. "Where were you earlier?"

She shrugs. "I told you. I was here, waiting for you."

I've been around this block twenty times tonight. This is the first time I've seen her. "Did you take up painting?"

The truth lies in her eyes. Or should I say the lies. It's the same look I'd get when I'd ask her about moving in together, or her job prospects in town so she could stick around.

"You need to come down to the station. There are some officers who'd like to talk to you about your aim with a paintball gun."

Red and blue lights reflect off the glass of the storefront, and I glance over my shoulder to see Patrice shrugging.

"You can't arrest me. You have no proof that I've done anything wrong." She squirms to get out of my hold.

I'm sure her assumption is that I'd let her go because in her mind, I'm probably still stupidly in love with her. I can't deny there's still a soft spot there, but I no longer pine over her like a sappy schmuck.

"I'm not gonna argue with you Leilani." I grab my hand-cuffs and secure them on her wrists.

"What are you gonna do? Take me up to your apartment with these cuffs on? Just like the old days, huh?"

"No." I try not to let the visual she's so eager to produce in my mind come to fruition.

I turn her toward the cruiser and Leilani balks. "Seriously, the lights? Why not put your siren on too?" At least she finally realizes this is serious.

Patrice isn't even trying to bite down her smile as I walk Leilani back to the squad car, open the door, and press my hand on her head to lower her in.

"Hello, Leilani," Patrice says.

"Patrice."

As I round the back of the car, I catch sight of all my friends on the balcony. I assume Rian must've alerted them. My gaze falls to Rian on the sidewalk outside her shop, her hand covering her mouth and a look of sorrow in her eyes.

I hate that damn look.

"Go back inside, Rian," I say and climb into the driver's side.

Just to be a dick, I turn on the sirens, but it's me who'll suffer for this. Move on over, Ben—I'm the new joke at the station now.

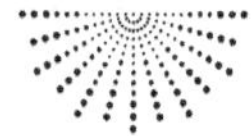

CHAPTER TWO

Knox

"I think you're the first to have to arrest your girlfriend," DuPont says, snickering with Milliken as they pass by my desk.

"Ex-girlfriend," Patrice says, but she's talking to air because they're busy spreading the gossip.

Back when we were an item, I brought Leilani to the precinct's Christmas party and to a wedding for an officer at the station. So when Captain Donnelly saw me walk her into the station in cuffs, his chin fell to his chest. I've never been more embarrassed in my life—except for that time back in fourth grade when I stuttered my way through my read-aloud session and got stuck with the shitty tagline of "Knox is as dumb as a box of rocks."

At the moment, Leilani is with the detectives and in a room where she's out of my sight.

"How did you ever meet her in the first place?" Patrice asks, tapping her pen on the desk across from mine.

I shake my head, remembering that night for the first time in a long time. Leilani has weaved in and out of my life so often that I never really think about the first time we met. But the way I would describe it is that she flew into my life rather than walked in.

"We were at this bar named Duke's. Me, Dylan, and a few other guys. There was this table of girls nearby that we started talking to."

"Leilani was one of them?" Patrice asks over a stack of papers as she moves to the other side of her desk.

I shake my head. "No. They were friends with the waitress."

I smile, remembering the waitress. She was Polynesian, just like Leilani. I'd been flirting with the waitress originally.

"Waitress?"

I nod. "She was waiting on us the entire night and brought us some drinks from her friends. One of them was into Dylan."

"What's not to be into?"

I raise my eyebrows. "You're married."

"And he's engaged. Doesn't mean I can't appreciate a good-looking guy."

Shaking my head, I continue. "She had this smile that lit up the entire room. She was sweet and funny and—"

"Was Leilani the waitress?"

"No. Leilani came later. I'd just forgotten about that waitress until you brought this up."

Patrice's eyebrows furrow as she stares at me as though she wants me to get to the point.

"I'd been talking with the waitress most of the night, flirting, and I was gonna ask her what she was doing when she got off. But one of my friends was saying she was like the girl next door. You know, the kind that you bring home to your mother. That set off the alarm bells in my head."

"Men are such jackasses." Patrice opens a drawer at her desk and grabs a Snickers bar, opens the wrapper, and takes a big bite.

I shrug. "I was young. Like… twenty-three? The last thing I wanted was something serious. Someone who'd want to meet my mother. Someone who'd be weighing my capability of taking care of them for the rest of their life. So I came to my senses when my friend said it. Then the door opened, and Leilani blew in."

Patrice sighs. "Let's not make it sound like a romance movie. You didn't live happily ever after, remember? You just arrested her."

"I know, I know. But I was blown away by her demeanor. Like she was there to party and live life as it came to her instead of having some predestined plan of what she wanted."

"And now she shoots people with paint guns."

I hear Patrice, but my mind is still at that bar. I'm thinking about that waitress and the path my life might have traveled if I'd asked her out instead of hooking up with Leilani.

"She won you over in bed, didn't she?"

I scoff, but Patrice is right. Leilani isn't one for inhibitions, and she's as comfortable with her sexuality as she is with her place in this world. I'd never met someone without *any* insecurities, and I always felt like I fell short. Because growing up poor as shit with people thinking you're dumb as rocks leaves a mark. But I kept those parts of me hidden from Leilani and only showed her the strong personality people tend to expect from a police officer.

"Anyway, I think we dated for, like, three months that first time. I guess maybe I wouldn't even call it dating. More like one of us would call the other when we wanted to have sex. Then she left for some march or something in DC. Never returned. Came back six months later or so, and that time we actually started dating." I shake my head, not wanting to relive this memory. "She came and went multiple times. The last time she stayed longer than she ever had before and I thought she'd settled down, but I was wrong."

"Man, you really screwed that up." Patrice balls up her Snickers wrapper and tosses it in the trash can.

I straighten in my chair and roll up to my desk. "She left me, not the other way around."

"I'm talking about the waitress. You should've dated her. She seems more your speed."

"Actually, wanna know something strange? Leilani came in that night to see the waitress, but in all the times I met her friends, I never saw that waitress again. That's odd, right?"

"Everything about the chick is odd," Patrice says.

Another good point. I can't help but wonder whatever happened to that waitress and if she's even still friends with Leilani.

An hour later, we've finished our report on Leilani's arrest and Patrice has gone home, but I pretend I have a million things to do just so I can find out what's going to happen to Leilani. I shouldn't give a shit, but I can't help myself.

I head to the men's room only to see the giant yellow sign saying it's closed.

"Milliken clogged it again," DuPont says as he passes by. "Hey, what's going on with your girlfriend? Maybe they'll let you fingerprint her."

"Damn Milliken," I mutter, heading out to the lobby.

As soon as I step through the door from the back, a woman rushes through the front doors of the station and over to our desk clerk, Mac. "My friend was arrested. I think she's here. She called me and told me to come down."

My hand stills on the men's bathroom door. I haven't heard that voice in many years, but for whatever reason, I recognize it. It's that waitress from the night I met Leilani.

Instead of eavesdropping, I go into the bathroom, but the entire time I take a piss and wash my hands, my mind is on what's happening on the other side of the doors. When I emerge, she's still there. She turns as the men's room door shuts, and our gazes meet.

Damn, one thing I forgot was how beautiful she is. How did I forget that? Probably because Leilani's like a hurricane and all you remember is how she careened into your life.

"You," she says, walking across the old linoleum to me. "You're Leilani's guy, no?"

What lies has Leilani been spouting?

"No." I shake my head.

Her hands raise and she squints one eye as she thinks of my name. Finally, her vision lands on my nameplate. "Whelan. Um…"

"Knox."

She snaps her fingers. "Yes. So are you going to help her?"

"No."

Her shoulders fall. "Why not? She called me and said she'd probably need bail money."

"Do you know what she did?"

"She said she didn't do anything. That it's all a misunderstanding."

I laugh. "The desk clerk can help you." I slide by her to disappear into the back, but before I open the door, I turn around to give the girl some advice. "I wouldn't bail her out. You'll never see that money again."

She tucks her long dark hair behind her ears. She's wearing yoga pants and a waist-length, tight-fitting sweatshirt that shows off her curves. This woman looks better than good, but she also has another look about her. The one that says, "I'm the savior, the helper, the mother hen of all my friends."

"She's innocent. She said she was."

"I wouldn't believe her."

Mac's head swivels in my direction. "Whelan, I've got this."

I raise my hands. "By all means." I square my gaze on the waitress one last time. "You might as well take that money and rip it into shreds right here. She's never going to change."

Her dark eyes narrow and she glances at Mac before stomping over to me. She pokes her finger into my chest. "What is your problem? Are you always such an asshole?"

I'll make this easy on both of us. "Yes."

I open the door and leave her behind like the first time I met her.

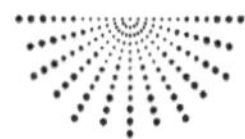

CHAPTER THREE

Kamea

*L*eilani comes out of the police station mid-afternoon and falls into me, wrapping me in a hug. "Thank you so much, Kam. I can't believe my ex-boyfriend arrested me. I mean seriously, right?"

"Yeah, the guy's an asshole. I ran into him in the lobby."

"He's a different person at work." She waves off the topic of her ex. "Mind if we grab some food? I'm starved."

How can she be worried about eating? She was just arrested. "Leilani, what's happening? Do you need a lawyer?"

I don't want to be insensitive, but I want to ask her when she plans on paying me back like she said she would during her one phone call. She called me out of the blue two nights ago, asking for a place to stay. Then she showed up with two men in tow. Who knows when their brilliant plan to shoot paintballs at women wearing fur coats while coming out of the country club came to mind. Though the idea probably came from when they met me at the country club on my last day of work before it closed for six months for renovations.

"No. They have no proof. It's all circumstantial."

"What about Wade and Paul? Did they get caught too?"

She glances back at the police station and clings to my arm tighter, turning us around the corner. "No, and you can't tell anyone that we were planning on doing it, okay?"

"I don't want to be involved in this." I really should've listened to my gut two nights ago when she called. What was I thinking? I was thinking I owed her.

I sure regret that decision now. Especially since things with Leilani always end disastrously. I don't have enough fingers to count how many times I've been uncomfortable with her ideas of fun. She's a do-good girl fighting for climate control, animal rights, and many causes I hold dear to my heart too, but I don't point a paintball gun at the people who disagree.

"Did you hear about the guy?" She snickers. "He ended up in the hospital. His balls are like melons." She leans forward, giggling as if she can hardly contain herself.

And again, I wonder how I got here. How I just spent the money I saved over two years for my T-shirt company on a bulk order to send to the screen-printer. Now it's in the government's bank account until she shows up to court for her hearing. And I don't even have my part time job at the country club anymore to subsidize my T-shirt endeavor.

"When do you see the judge again?" I ask as she opens the door of Los Tacos.

"Can we please talk about this after we eat? The food is shit in there. I couldn't even force myself to eat it." She tells the hostess that there's only two of us and soon we're seated. "Hey, you don't mind spotting me for lunch, do you?"

"Leilani, I love you, but—"

"You're the best. Thanks." She picks up her menu and looks it over. "I promise I'll pay you back."

"Hey." I put my finger on the edge of the menu and push it down so I can see her face. "I need the money I posted for your bail. Remember last night before your escapade when you came into my room, asking what I was doing? Remember the T-shirt company I run? Remember all the cute sayings we came up with?"

"Oh yeah, that was fun. I miss times like that with you." Her hand extends over the free chips and salsa, and she pats my arm.

"Yeah, and I can't place my bulk T-shirt order unless I have the money that I just used for your bail."

She places her menu down and takes a chip, dipping it in the salsa. "Don't even worry about it. Wade owes me money. And after me taking the blame, he'll pay you back."

The waitress comes over and we order.

"Okay, because—"

"I said I've got you. What? You don't trust me?" She looks deeply offended.

My face heats for questioning her, guilt weighing heavy on my shoulders. "No, I do. It's just—"

"Then can we please talk about how my ex-boyfriend— the guy who begged me to marry him—arrested me this morning? How could he do that?" She dips a chip, this time bowling the salsa inside her chip. The waitress brings over her margarita. "Oh, you're an angel."

Leilani wastes no time putting her lips over the small straw and sucking in so much, I'm surprised the cup isn't dry once she's finished.

"He proposed to you?" This is the first I'm hearing of this.

I'd never bring this up to Leilani, but years ago when she first met Knox, I'd thought maybe I'd be going home with him that night. But just like every guy we went to high school with, as soon as he saw Leilani, I was old news. A crazy "I'm up for anything and live on the edge" kind of girl is hard for most guys to resist.

She nods while chewing a chip. "How did he ever think I'd wanna be married? I mean, I like the guy but..."

"Like? Didn't you date him for a long time?"

She shrugs, and I decide I don't really want to talk about Knox or her relationship with him. The whole situation reminds me of that night we first met him and brings my insecurities to the surface.

Without giving her an opportunity to answer—from the way she's shoving chips in her mouth, she didn't plan on responding to my question anyway—I return to my original question. "When is your court date?"

Her lips purse. "I think next month or something."

I roll my eyes as the waitress brings over our meals. "Do you think your parents could pay me the money back?"

She stops the fork filled with enchilada from entering her mouth and gives me the death stare of all death stares. I'm sure she's wondering how I could suggest involving her parents.

"I need the money," I say, almost pleading. "I'm sorry. I know you don't want to talk about it, but I've been saving for two years for this opportunity."

"Is this the T-shirt thing again? I mean, come on. Are you really going to make a living selling a few T-shirts?"

She has no idea how much I've been selling with print-on-demand, but to get my cost per unit down and get orders out faster, I have to be in control of my inventory. And for that to happen, I have to have the actual shirts.

I push away my tacos and grab my water. My appetite's gone sour now. "I get that you're willing to just live out of a suitcase, but I'm not."

She wipes her mouth and looks into her lap for a

moment. "Kam, I totally appreciate you fronting the money. I'd never expect you to go without. I'll talk to Wade and get it for you. Don't worry. And I live out of a suitcase because I choose to. I'm always up for anything."

I nod because I get it. Guilt still lives inside me over what caused her to run away in the first place, but I think she enjoys her life now. No strings, no complications.

We finish eating, me more picking while Leilani cleans her plate. I pay the check and her attitude does a one-eighty as she thanks me profusely. It isn't until we're outside my small studio apartment in the neighboring town of Peekskil that the real ramifications of Leilani coming back into my life hits me.

"You can't just kick her out," Leilani screams at my landlord as I stare at all my belongings sitting on the sidewalk outside my building. If it weren't a furnished apartment I was renting, would my couch and mattress be out here too?

"Can and did. She violated the lease and the property owner doesn't give second chances." She crosses her arms over her large chest.

"A noise complaint?" Leilani asks. "Come on."

Wade and Paul stand on the corner, smoking cigarettes and looking completely unfazed that they got me kicked out of my apartment.

According to Sally, my building manager—who I thought had my back—Paul and Wade had an afternoon party, and Paul and his other delinquent buddies decided to skateboard down the handrails of the stairway, one of them falling right through the glass-paned door.

I run my hand down my face. "Sally, you know it wasn't me."

"You're just a spiteful bitch!" Leilani screams.

I put my hands on her shoulders and shove her toward Wade and Paul. She goes reluctantly, spitting out more names at Sally.

Sally's a hard nut and it took me at least six months before she even gave me more than a nod when we ran into one another. Over the two years I've lived here, I thought we had established a mutual respect for one another.

"I'm sorry. They're gone, and I won't allow them to come back," I say.

Sally looks down the sidewalk toward them and shakes her head. "I wish I could give you a second chance, but Mr. Henderson already wanted to call the police. This is a quiet building, Kamea, and I can't afford to lose this managerial position. It's out of my hands."

She means the situation has already been addressed by the owner of the property, Dick Jagoff, otherwise known as Richard Geoff. The man is a complete narcissist with no empathy. I called once to say I would be late with the rent but that I'd have it in two days. He put an eviction sticker on my door. According to him, it was his way of embarrassing me into never being late with my rent again. He's a bully in a velvet tracksuit. I could fight this, I'm sure he's violated my lease himself not giving me any notice before evicting me but that all takes time and money—neither of which I have.

"If you want to keep your stuff at my place until you find somewhere permanent"—she looks around as though Dick will turn the corner any minute—"you can."

I look at my television. I don't have a ton of stuff, but enough that I can't transport it by myself.

"Thanks. I appreciate that. I'll stay with a friend, but as soon as I land a new place, I'll grab everything."

Glancing over my shoulder at Leilani and the guys, I see the corner where they were standing is now vacant. I sigh and collect everything but a suitcase that Sally packed for me with all my clothes, and my laptop bag. I'd pawn it for money if I didn't need it for the T-shirt business.

After I load all of my belongings into Sally's apartment, I say, "Thanks again."

She nods and touches my upper arm. "That girl is bad news. You need to cut ties because she's only gonna drag you down."

I offer a smile because her heart is in the right place. It's not the first time I've heard that about Leilani, but she's my friend. And she saved me once. Maybe I'm trying to repay her by saving her in turn. I'm also aware that I'm the reason she ran to begin with. If it hadn't been for that horrible night, she might not be who she is now.

"I'll be in touch."

Sally scowls and shakes her head as though I didn't really hear her warning.

With my suitcase heavy in my hand and my laptop bag swung over my shoulder, I walk toward the corner where Leilani was. I need that money from Wade now more than I did an hour ago. He owes me for getting me evicted.

But I don't see the three of them anywhere nearby. I pull my phone out of my purse and dial Leilani's number, but it goes to voicemail after only one ring. Maybe it's dead. I leave a message for her to call me as soon as she gets it.

Realizing I can't stand here forever, I dial up my only other friend, who happens to be my boss from the country club. A train ride later, I'm back in Cliffton Heights and my boss, Chris, is waiting for me with his four boys running on the sidewalk, trying to beat the train.

"It'll only be one night," I grumble.

He nods. "Didn't think I'd see you until the spring when the renovations are complete." He smiles. "And don't worry about it. You can stay as long as you need to."

"Thanks."

One of the boys jumps on my back and another attaches to my leg. Another one can't stop telling me about the booger he just pulled out of his nose before I arrived.

When will I ever learn my lesson when it comes to Leilani?

CHAPTER FOUR

Knox

I walk out of the locker room and into the station at the start of my shift, cracking my neck back and forth, shutting and opening my eyes. This overnight shift is kicking my ass lately and just another reminder why I want that detective position.

Patrice is already at her desk. We'll have to go into the call room in five minutes, but I sit down anyway. Leilani's mugshot is taped to my computer with a big heart drawn in red Sharpie around her face. I tear off the photo and throw it in the trash. Surprisingly, Patrice says nothing.

"Fucking hell," I say.

"You know that's not the last of it?" Patrice says.

"I know." I run my hands down my face.

Having Leilani show up here two days ago has spurred a clusterfuck in my brain, but it's also solidified that I'm done with her for good. A reckless person who would go after someone with a paint gun just because the woman wore a fur coat is not the woman for me, among other reasons.

Although I'd prefer to be getting a good night's sleep, at least I'm processing how different we are.

Patrice stands, tucks in her chair, and the two of us head to the call room before we'll head out to the squad cars. The captain talks about the two male suspects who have yet to be picked up from the Bruce Floyd attack. Apparently, Floyd wants their heads on a platter. A man like Bruce Floyd is used to getting what he wants when he wants it, and I'm sure the captain is getting a shit-ton of pressure to get it done. I'm not sure I ever want to get that high up the ranks.

We all file out of the room, DuPont slapping me on the back. "Try not to arrest any of your other girlfriends."

He and Milliken think they're funny as they walk away laughing and glancing back for my reaction.

"I heard the thirteenth precinct has an opening for a spring wedding," another guy says.

"Black and white stripes are in," another coworker adds.

"Glad to see I'm the butt of all jokes." I'm not surprised though. It's going to be me until someone else does something stupid.

"Whelan!" Captain Donnelly calls.

Patrice's eyes widen. She hasn't made one smart joke herself, which is odd.

"Hey, Cap," I say.

"I want to talk to you before you leave after your shift, so check in with me." He never looks up from his papers at the podium.

I hope it has something to do with the detective position and not my ex being arrested. "Yes, sir."

He grabs his papers and heads to his office, nodding at me like that's all.

When I reach the car, I realize it's Patrice's turn to drive. I place my hands together in prayer and she looks at me with no amusement before she heads to the driver's side. We both slide in and head out.

"Cap wants to talk to me," I say.

"You do know that I'm gonna be pissed off at you when you make detective. Who knows who my new partner might be?"

She turns toward the bridges where homeless people often hang out. Most of the homeless are decent people, but there are thieves too. They tend to live by their own rules since no one wants to involve the police in their matters for fear they'll be taken in.

"Then try for detective too," I say.

"But then I'd be detective and you'd still be a beat cop." She grins at me.

I chuckle. "No doubt."

Patrice doesn't have as many years of experience as I do, but she'd make a great detective someday and I wouldn't mind continuing our partnership. She's the only one I don't mind giving me hell.

"So tell me, are you thinking of her?"

And she also thinks my love life is up for discussion at all times. She's like a nagging mother, except that she's three years younger than me.

"Nah, I told you, I'm over her."

She turns again, this time returning the way we came but going slower, both of us looking for anything unusual. "Yeah, those bags under your eyes are evidence of that."

The worst part about having a woman partner is she sees and hears everything. If I have a two-second phone conversation, she can figure out who it was and what they wanted.

"I'm processing, but I don't want her back if that's what you want to know."

"Hey, your business is your business."

"Uh-huh. Sure," I say.

As she slows, I squint at a spot under the overpass. "Slow up."

Patrice eases off the gas and we inch along. "What is it?"

I peek forward, rolling down my window.

"This is mine!" Dell, a homeless woman every cop knows because she panhandles on corners all the time, yells. "Get out of my spot."

"I don't see your name on it," someone else says.

The only reason I can make out Dell is her signature neon yellow hat. The other person I don't know. Then a suitcase tumbles down the cement incline, opening up and spilling someone's belongings.

"Hold up," I say, and Patrice presses on the brakes and flicks the lights. "We don't need lights."

"You're not Spiderman, Knox. You're not protecting Cliffton Heights in a mask. There are protocols."

Patrice is right, but as I suspected would happen, the homeless population scatters, except for the veterans like Dell. And whoever she's yelling at.

I shine my flashlight up there. "Dell, come on down."

She blows out a breath. "She's in my spot. This is my spot on Wednesdays and Fridays."

"There's no name on the spot," a woman's voice says.

Dell shakes her head and moves a foot to the right, allowing me to see the woman she's talking to. My stomach sinks when I see her face. A million questions flicker to mind.

"You." I leave the flashlight on her. "Come down here."

Her shoulders fall and she grabs another bag before walking down the incline, picking up her discarded items on the way. She doesn't come to me right away, but instead she goes to her suitcase and packs it back up. "I didn't do anything."

"What are you doing here?" I ask.

"What does it look like? I was trying to sleep, or at least have shelter from the wind, when Dolly Parton came in, demanding that I move."

I bite the inside of my cheek so I don't smile. I shift my flashlight up at Dell who is now lying down. "Dell, you're not clear of this. Come on down."

She flips me off. I glance at Patrice in the car—who might as well have a bowl of popcorn in her lap, she's so fascinated by what's happening. Maybe she should get out of the car. I aim my flashlight back at Leilani's friend.

She puts up her hand. "Can you please turn that thing off? Did you miss the streetlight?"

She points, and sure enough, now that she's down here, I don't need it as much. I click off the flashlight and put it back in my holster.

"I'm going to ask you again, why are you here?"

"And I'm going to answer again with why the hell do you think?"

Damn, she's got attitude. The problem with attitude on a hot woman is that it turns me the fuck on. Always has. I've always dated the girls who don't teeter on that line but are so far over it, they don't give a fuck what anyone thinks. I've broken up more than my fair share of fights between chicks. In fact, my first ever girlfriend got more detentions than any other girl in the school. Understandably, I'm trying my hardest not to be attracted to this woman.

"You just bailed out Leilani, so I know you aren't broke."

She crawls around the cement, snagging her clothing, until she's right at my feet. Unbeknownst to me, a piece of skimpy lingerie lies on top of my boots. It's pink with lace and looks like I could tear it apart with my pinkies.

Damn it. I'm officially turned on thinking about her

wearing it and me ripping it to shreds while pulling it off her body.

"It's a long story, okay?"

"Where is she?" I ask because it's clear this girl isn't normally calling an overpass home. She's the kind who works her ass off for what's hers.

"Oh, your one true love?" she sneers.

I rear back, thinking I might hear jealousy in her tone. "Leilani."

"Same thing, isn't it?" She zips up her suitcase and stands with it on its wheels. "See you later, Whelan." She walks down the street.

I follow, and Patrice inches the squad car along with us. I hold my hand to tell Patrice to lay off, but she doesn't listen. She never fucking listens. Who needs a wife when I have my partner?

"Stop following me, otherwise I'll call the..." The girl stops speaking.

I chuckle. "The cops?"

She whirls around, and those sweet chocolate eyes that lured me to her that night we first met are practically flaming with anger. "Don't think I won't go above your head. I get that you're the type who likes to save women and all that, but I don't need saving. I'm fine." She turns back around and stomps off.

"And that's why you're outside in the middle of winter, trying to sleep in a flimsy coat? Let me take you to a shelter at least."

She flips me off and keeps walking. I shrug at Patrice, who is actually eating another Snickers bar as we move along the dark, vacant street during the early hours of the morning when everyone else is sleeping.

"What do you want from me?" The girl flips around to face me again.

"I just want to get you somewhere safe."

Her eyes scan my body. Not in an "I want to bang you" way, but more like she might be a second from cracking and she's willing herself to stay strong. I've seen this type of behavior plenty of times. She's not the hard-ass she pretends to be. If she was, she would've deserted her suitcase or worse, tried to throw a punch at me.

Her eyes steady on me and her shoulders fall like they did moments ago at the top of the overpass. "Leilani skipped out on me. The bail was everything I have. And worse, her friends got me kicked out of my apartment. I've tried to call her, and she won't answer. I was staying with my boss, but he's got four boys and a wife. After they threw flour all over me in the shower as their fifth prank that day, I left."

"Boys can be cruel," I say, ignoring all the shit that Leilani left in her wake.

She nods. "But I don't need your help, okay? I'll figure this out."

"Okay," I say, stepping forward, my hand on her upper arm.

"What are you doing?"

"I'm dropping you off at my place. You can spend the night there." She tries to get free of my grip, but I only hold it harder. "I have an extra room. You can stay tonight, and when I get off work, we'll figure something out."

"I am not your problem. Will you stop?" She squirms, but I open the car's back door.

Patrice shoots me a look I know is trying to communicate that I shouldn't try to be someone else's savior. But shit, if I didn't get into policing to help people, why the fuck am I doing this job?

I release the girl's arm but stand in front of her. "Listen, I'm not trying to fix your problems, but you can't stay out here. It's not safe, and my captain wouldn't be too happy if I just parked the squad car here all night. I'm a cop and I was sworn to uphold the law, and I cannot leave you here like this. You won't fare well. So just do me the favor and stay at my place. I won't even be there."

She takes a moment to think about it and nods without another word. I hold open the back door and she crawls in. I stuff her suitcase in next to her.

Once I'm in, Patrice puts the car in drive. "Where to?"

"My apartment."

"You know her?" she asks me.

"This is one of Leilani's friends. I met her once when she was a waitress."

Her eyebrows scrunch and I know what she's thinking. I don't need telepathy to figure it out. She surprises me though and turns around to look in the back seat. "I'm Patrice, and you are?"

"Kamea," she says.

That's right, Kamea is her name.

Thank you, Patrice. I guess sometimes her interfering actually helps.

CHAPTER FIVE

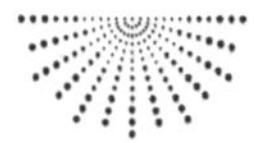

Kamea

My face still stings hot with embarrassment as we pull up in front of Knox's apartment building.

"It was nice meeting you," Patrice says. She was sweet as can be the entire ride, telling stories about the woman, Dell, who was so adamant about me being in her space.

"Thanks."

Knox takes my bag, and I couldn't feel more like a damsel in distress right now. I hate owing anyone anything, but I couldn't stay at Chris's anymore. Those boys never left me alone, and it was clear his wife wasn't as cool with me being there as he was. Especially when I heard them fighting and she asked if he was fucking me. It's not a situation I want to be a part of.

I thought one night outside wouldn't kill me. Surely, I could handle one night outside until I figured something out.

But as I was drifting to sleep, that woman got in my face. If Knox hadn't shown up, what would I have done? Asked someone for directions to a shelter, I guess.

Knox didn't seem like the type to give up and let me leave without taking him up on his offer, so I decided I'll sleep at his place for the rest of the night, then I'll leave before he even gets off his shift.

"When do you get home?" I ask as he inserts his key into the lock of his apartment door.

The hallway is so quiet, the key going into the hole sounds as loud as a gun going off. He glances at me and opens the door fully. "Don't try to run, I'll find you."

"Thank you for letting me stay," I say, ignoring his comment and following him into the small apartment.

"You can sleep in here. My one roommate just moved out, and his new girlfriend demanded they buy a new bed, so..." He flicks on the light. It's a bare room with white walls. There's a bed, sans headboard, pushed against the wall and an old chair in the corner. "I have another roommate, Jax, but he's probably asleep right now. Just shut the door when you go to the bathroom or shower."

A hot shower sounds so nice, but I tell my achy body it's not getting that pleasure right now.

"Towels are in the hall closet, and we share food. Jax is cool, so he won't care if you eat anything." Knox hovers by the door. "I'm off at seven, but I probably won't be back until eight or so. Just sleep and I'll bring some coffee with me when I come back." He looks like he wants to say more, but he doesn't.

"Thanks again, I owe you for this."

He shakes his head. "No, you don't. Let's just say I understand. But I did warn you not to bail her out. You obviously didn't have the money to spare."

"Thanks, Dad," I snip.

His lips purse and he rocks back on his shoes. "See you around eight."

Then he leaves before I can apologize. I should've bitten my tongue before sassing him. He's letting me stay in his apartment.

After I hear the front door shut and he locks it from the other side, I do what any girl would do—I check out the place. I open the fridge, surprised by how stocked it is. Their pantry is as well—mostly junk food but food, nonetheless. My stomach grumbles, so I shut the cabinet and move into the bathroom. Peeking into the shower, I see it's filled with men's products. Every item has some woodsy or ocean scent. Their medicine cabinet holds the typical pain relievers, heartburn medicine, etc.

What kind of bachelors are these guys? I was expecting a fridge full of beer and a medicine cabinet full of condoms.

Then I bend down and open the lower cabinets and see my first sign that bachelors do in fact live in this apartment. They must buy their condoms at Costco.

"Shit, am I dreaming?" a rough-sounding voice says from the open doorway.

My head whips around and my gaze flies to his. Jax, I presume, stands there in white boxer briefs, one hand on his face, the other scratching his chest. He's hot, covered with tattoos, and not nearly as muscular as Knox, but more lean-muscled. One of his nipples is pierced and he flashes me a wicked smile that says these condoms are probably well-used by him.

"No. Sorry, Knox is letting me stay here, but I'll head back to my room and you can do your business."

I slide out of the bathroom and he doesn't move, which means my breasts run along his bare arm.

"Don't run off, Little Red Riding Hood. I'm not the Big

Bad Wolf." He chuckles at his own joke and heads into the bathroom.

I wait for the door to shut, but it doesn't and the sound of him peeing rings through the quiet apartment. Water runs from the faucet afterward. At least he practices good hand hygiene, I guess. I back up toward the bedroom. I should've just locked myself inside.

But the guy heads to the kitchen, speaking to me. "I'm Jax." He opens the fridge and grabs a water, holding it up in offer to me.

"Sure. Thanks."

He throws it at me, and I barely catch it out of surprise. Most people would just hand it to someone. I'm about to step through the doorway of the bedroom I'm staying in when he clears his throat. I glance over my shoulder and he eyes the couch. What is with this guy?

"Knox doesn't usually pick up strays except for me and our buddy Dylan. What's your story?"

I don't want to judge, but Jax doesn't look like someone who really cares about someone's backstory. He looks like the guy who lives his life how he wants, and people who get in his way are just nuisances to be dealt with.

"He's just helping me out for the night."

"What's your name?"

I fidget with the water bottle. "Kamea."

He nods. "Cool. Sit down. I've been struggling to sleep lately, and now that I'm up, I'm bored."

I eye the game console. "Play a game?"

"Are you saying you don't wanna talk to me?"

My stomach growls, and since there's no other sound in the apartment, Jax laughs. He heads to the freezer, pulls out a frozen pizza, and pre-heats the oven.

"Oh, I'm not—"

"No. I am." He never looks at me.

What is with these guys? Knox gives me a room to sleep and this guy is making me pizza in the middle of the night.

"'Cause I'm not hungry."

He nods. "So you said. But I am."

I let it go.

"How about I start this get-to-know-each-other session and if you feel like saying anything, you can."

"Start what?" I ask.

"I'm a tattoo artist." His gaze falls over my body. "I'm thinking you don't have a tattoo."

Joke's on this guy. Like everyone else, he thinks I'm a good girl and there's nothing more to me. I pull up the sleeve of my sweatshirt to show him the three lines around my forearm.

He nods, looking impressed. "Awesome, what are the lines symbolic for?"

"Why would I tell you?"

He holds up his hands. "Yeah, you don't have to tell me, but next tattoo, you come to me. That fill-in looks like shit."

I roll my eyes. "Yeah, okay." I lower my sleeve.

"I work at Ink Envy, and I've known Knox since he was a virgin. Unfortunately for me, my buddy Dylan lives across the hall with his girl, Rian, and we have two friends who live down the hall who are shacked up too. And another girl who's with a damn prince." He holds up his hand before I can say something. "I can't make this shit up. I was a foster kid who bounced around my whole life. I come here to ground myself for a bit and I end up surrounded by all these people who think love is real and shit."

"And you don't?" I crack open the bottle and sip the cool water. The oven beeps and he puts the pizza inside.

"Believe in love?" He huffs. "I'm not saying my friends aren't in love. They probably are, and they look happy and shit. Don't get me wrong. But... I don't know. Maybe it's not for me. I can't even conceive of someone depending on me, let alone trusting someone enough to open up my chest and let my heart fall out. As if they could heal all the cuts and scrapes I've collected over the years…" He shakes his head. "I guess I have a hard time buying it, is all." He looks me over again. "You look like you like rom-coms and shit."

I sit on the recliner, propping one leg up. This is the weirdest exchange I've ever had with a guy. At the same time, I'm fascinated. "I do like rom-coms, but I also like thrillers and a little sci-fi."

"But you believe in true love and shit?"

"Um… yeah, I guess. Doesn't every girl believe there's someone out there for her?"

"I can name you one for sure who doesn't. Visit me down at Ink Envy and I'll introduce you." He chuckles and slides onto the stool by the breakfast bar.

"I think it comes down to people being scared of getting hurt. Love makes you vulnerable. It forces you to open the gate to that space where you hide your true self, allowing the other person to see the real you and to judge what they see. Sometimes people don't take that seriously and you get hurt. I think the gate gets heavier every time you trust someone, and they fail you."

He nods then pretends to swipe a tear. "Damn, girl, I just asked if you like rom-coms."

I throw my water cap at him and he catches it, laughing as he hops off the stool.

"Can you please put on some pants?"

He looks down at himself as though he forgot he wasn't wearing anything but boxers. He seems the type who's comfortable in his own body. "I'd thought maybe we could screw so we could both fall asleep after, but I can tell you're here for Knox."

He disappears into his room before I can explain how

dead wrong he is. He returns wearing a pair of gray sweat-pants as the buzzer of the oven goes off.

"Knox had his shot and he chose Leilani." I don't know why I say it.

Jax glances at me and our eyes catch. His silent question and my nod. It's more information than I intended to give the guy, but hey, why not lay out all the cards? I'll never see him again after tonight.

"Fuck!" He pulls his hand back from the oven and sucks on his finger.

I scramble up and usher him to the faucet, where I turn on the cold water and shove his hand underneath. Once he's situated, I get the pizza out of the oven, then turn it off.

"Shocked you, did I?"

"You kinda look like her now that you mention Leilani. You're not…"

"Sisters?" I laugh, and he nods. "No. We're both Polyne-sian though, and our hair is basically the same. Our families are friends. We were neighbors growing up."

He turns off the faucet then sucks on his finger again. "Are you in contact with her? Because I'm not really—"

"No, her friends got me kicked out of my apartment. I bailed her out after she was arrested, only for her to disap-pear on me. Knox found me under an overpass tonight and he offered to let me spend the night here."

His body language changes. "Well, shit. That sucks."

I nod and search the drawers for a pizza cutter to keep myself busy before I break down over the situation I find myself in.

He shrugs. "Stay here as long as you want. Knox and I cover the rent just fine."

"You're crazy. I'm leaving before Knox gets home tomorrow."

He raises his eyebrows. "Tell me more about when Knox had a chance with you."

"Why?"

He opens the cabinet where paper plates are, and I grab two. Thankfully he says nothing about my earlier disclaimer that I wasn't hungry.

"Because I have insomnia from not getting laid because of some crappy bet I'm in and you should have sympathy for me. Plus, I made you a pizza. And overall, I'm a cool guy. I'll even throw in a tattoo."

I laugh, and it stops him from spewing more bullshit. "Fine. Let's at least get comfortable, and I'm throwing out a disclaimer right now—I do not want Knox Whelan, okay?"

"Whatever. I'm hoping the story is boring as fuck and I fall asleep."

And that's when I talk about a night I'm ashamed to admit I've thought of often since it happened, while Knox probably doesn't even remember it at all.

CHAPTER SIX

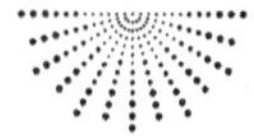

Knox

I slide into the squad car where Patrice is jamming to Salt-N-Pepa. Just when I think she's not paying attention, she squawks our radio outside of the car at two skateboarding kids who should be in bed.

"Aren't your mommas looking for you?" she yells through the radio.

One of the kids glances back and scurries around the corner, but the other one stops riding and taunts us with his steady glare.

"Man, kids have balls they didn't have when I was growing up," she says to me.

The kid eventually follows his friend. Usually I might've gotten out of the squad car and talked with him, but the whole debacle of having Leilani's friend in my apartment right now is messing with my mind. Two days ago, my life was good. Not great, but stress-free at least.

"So…" Patrice drags on the O and I know she's gonna want me to rehash this story all over again. "The waitress makes a reappearance, huh? Plot twist."

"Let's talk about Nate. What's he up to? Still looking to move you two to New York City?"

She laughs and drives down the road. "You're not getting off that easy, Whelan."

"You can't make me talk."

"I could hold a gun to your head."

My head flies her way and she laughs so hard I fear we're going to drive off the road. "Kidding. Of course."

I nod, but I'm not so sure. "Has anyone told you, you should've gone to school for psychology? Put some people on a couch and torment them?"

"Only you and Nate."

"Must be because you torture us the most."

She glances over and nods, a huge-ass smile on her face. "So what'll you do now that the waitress is back in town and Leilani's likely gonna have a warrant out for her arrest?"

I stare out the window into the darkness of Cliffton Heights. Leilani having a warrant out if she skips bail is my biggest problem. I feel bad for Kamea, but I'll never hear the end of Leilani's arrest from the guys at the station. Not to mention, I want the promotion to detective. Ex-girlfriend has a warrant issued after I arrested her? Not a good look.

I shrug. "I don't know."

Patrice says nothing for a few seconds, and I hope she's deciding a change of topic is necessary.

"I think a do-over is a good plan."

Should've guessed Patrice wouldn't take my cue about when she should leave shit alone.

"A do-over?"

"Yeah. I mean, the other day you had that look in your eye when you were talking about the waitress, and now, she's here, in your apartment. She could be naked right now in your bed."

"She's sleeping in Seth's old bed."

She huffs. "Get the point I'm making. Rarely do people get second chances. Maybe this is yours."

"First of all, I'm not gonna date anyone associated with Leilani, and second of all, I'm sure she just wants to get her money and go back to her life."

Patrice hums. That's my cue that she's annoyed or thinks she's right. Then again, Patrice always thinks she's right.

"Stop humming and let's finish this shift."

We get off duty in about two hours, and it's been slow other than Kamea thinking she was brave enough to sleep under an overpass. Patrice is right though—all I can think about is the night I first met Kamea and Leilani. That pull I felt to Kamea until Jimmy said she was more like the girl next door rather than a good time for the night. I'm ashamed now that a quick fuck was all I was looking for back then. I can't help but second-guess my decision that night, especially since Leilani weaving herself in and out of my life has screwed me over.

When our shift is almost done, Patrice and I walk into the station to file paperwork on a DUI we pulled over, and on my desk, I find a box with a black ribbon tied around it.

"A gift?" Patrice asks, sitting down and booting up her computer.

"Probably not a good one."

I untie the ribbon and open the box to find a save-the-date card printed on regular paper. There's a copy of Leilani's mug shot along with a picture of me in my uniform above words in big black bold lettering—**Metal bars can't even keep these two apart. Come witness them vow their undying love at Cliffton Heights Police Station. BYOBM – Bring Your Own Bail Money. Cash only. Thank you.**

I tear it up and shove it in the garbage.

DuPont walks by like he wasn't the mastermind behind it, but his smirk is so deep, it gives him away.

"You really need to kick his ass. You're double his size." Patrice types away on the computer.

"That will just add to my problems."

I've dealt with guys like DuPont and Milliken my entire life. They were the pricks making fun of me in elementary school for being "stupid." I kicked their asses in junior high after I grew six inches in height and three in width one summer. But I don't do that shit now. Not unless someone is hurting the ones I love.

"Whelan, get in here," Captain Donnelly calls from his office.

Patrice eyes me across the desk. "I got this."

I stand and head across the room to the captain's office. He's a stout man with a beer belly. Although he'd never be able to pass the physical test anymore, he doesn't have to. He's earned his stripes, and I've always enjoyed working under him.

"Shut the door," he says.

I do, and he points at the chair across from his desk. As I lower into the chair, I see the same box that was on my desk open on his. Fuck me. The other night when I brought Leilani in, all the captain did was shoot me a glare. I should've known he wouldn't let it slide.

"So." He links his hands over his strained belly and leans back in his chair. "Have anything you want to tell me?"

"That's bullshit. You know DuPont was responsible for it."

He holds up his hand to stop me and picks up another piece of paper from his desk. "This is your recommendation letter for the detective position. It's time, and I don't want something or someone to interfere in this again."

Yeah, you guessed it—Cap isn't really a fan of Leilani.

"I won't. The fact she's even back has nothing to do with me. I've washed my hands of her."

He nods. "And she didn't reach out after she was released? At least I saw that you didn't bail her out."

"No, her friend did."

He cocks one eyebrow. Yeah, if I was as detached as I'm saying, I wouldn't know that fact. He's right.

"I swear I'm not with her or even talking to her at all."

He lays the sheet of paper on the desk, leaning forward to intimidate me. Sweat forms at the base of my neck.

As if he's a human polygraph machine, he nods. "Then you won't mind finding someone else to bring to Louie's retirement party?"

I blink a couple of times. "What?"

"Show the big guys you've moved on. Remember when Leilani tried to hula dance at the Christmas party only to fall down on top of a table? People have long memories. The higher-ups even longer. You need to clear your name of her, and the best way to do that is to show you've moved on. I'm not saying you have to get married or even find a steady girlfriend. Just show people you're willing to let another woman into your life."

"So you're asking me to rent a date or something?"

He chuckles. "Don't you young people have that swipe right thing going on? Just find a date. You're a good-looking guy. I'm sure it can't be that hard."

I'm not opposed to bringing a woman to Louie's retirement party. Hell, I could ask one of the girls to come with me. With her sweet and innocent demeanor, Rian would be perfect. But there's still that damn part of me that hates being told what to do. I want to dig my feet in the ground and say I'm not gonna bring a date because you can't judge my ability to do a job on something irrelevant like that. I'm the most qualified candidate, so who cares who I'm dating?

"I'll find someone," I hear myself say, and the stubborn side of me kicks me in the ass for caving so easily.

He smiles. "See, that's why I've always liked you. You're a team player. Believe me, once they see you got a new girl, Leilani will be old news and the detective position will be yours."

I nod, unable to speak.

As I exit his office a few minutes later, I pull out my cell phone, knowing Rian is up and at the bakery.

Me: *Hey, can you come with me to a retirement party and pretend to be my girlfriend?*

Rian: *Sure. When is it?*

I sit at my desk, and Patrice hands me papers to sign and waits for me to tell her what happened.

"When is Louie's retirement party?" I ask.

She laughs. "Next Friday. Why?"

I shake my head.

Me: *Next Friday.*

Rian: *Oh sorry. All the girls are going into the city to see Blanca's dress.*

Me: *All of you guys?*

Rian: *Afraid so.*

I shut off my phone and sigh. Hell, this sucks.

"What did Cap say?" Patrice asks when I don't volunteer the information.

"Pull out your phone. I need a date for Louie's retirement party."

Her eyes light up. "My pleasure. Let me look through my Facebook friends list."

As her thumbs scroll down her screen, she pauses and looks at me. Her face bears that same expression it did when she thought someone should make s'mores using donuts. Trouble.

"What?"

"The waitress. She's cute and innocent looking. God knows she won't hula dance on the table."

I groan at the reminder of that night. The embarrassment of the situation as I walked Leilani out. The judging eyes on the back of my head. "I'm looking for something that doesn't complicate the situation further."

Patrice nods and buries her head in her phone again.

As we're walking out of the station later, Patrice says, "Sorry, I guess I thought I had more single friends. Turns out I don't." She shrugs.

"Thanks anyway." I'm not convinced she actually tried.

Nate honks his horn, interrupting us.

Patrice lingers by me instead of rushing over to her husband. "We're going to get some test results from our fertility doctor." She glances back at the station. "Don't tell anyone, okay?"

"I won't."

She beams and practically skips like a schoolgirl over to Nate. He raises his hand in a hello, and I do the same.

I can't help but feel as though everyone's life is moving forward and mine is stalled in neutral.

Fifteen minutes later, I insert the key into my apartment door, not sure what I'm about to find on the other side—but I can tell you, it isn't Kamea asleep with a shirtless Jax on the couch. That definitely wasn't on my radar.

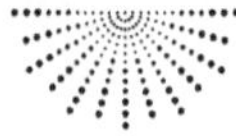

CHAPTER SEVEN

Kamea

A loud sound startles me awake and I jolt, my head hitting Jax's jaw.

"Motherfucker!" He quickly stands and grabs his chin. "Is your head made of steel?"

I rub my head and sit up straighter on the couch, realizing the sound must have been the door slamming. Knox stands just inside the apartment, looking at the two of us as though he's about to set fire to the place. It reads a lot like jealousy, but I have to be misreading that.

"Sorry, I'm not the one who slammed the door," I tell Jax.

Jax follows my vision to Knox. "What the fuck, man?"

"It slipped. I didn't think you two would be up already."

Jax cracks his neck. I can't deny he's attractive. He's got the bad boy vibe going on, with the tattoos and the cocky attitude that could make the most devoted church lady reveal her kinky side. But the fact that my cheek was apparently on his bare chest doesn't even excite me. Mostly because it's his roommate that's on my mind. But I can admire hot-blooded male perfection even if I don't want him.

Jax says, "Maybe shoot me a text next time you let a stranger stay in our apartment."

"I don't get texts every time you bring a stranger in. You know how many times I've been walked in on in the bathroom or shower?" Knox puts his bag on the kitchen chair and grabs orange juice from the fridge.

"Not in weeks." Jax heads to the bathroom. Again, he doesn't shut the door.

"Shut the door, dickwad, there's company," Knox yells.

"You mean he doesn't shut it when you're here either?" I ask, sliding onto a breakfast stool.

Knox grabs another cup and pours me orange juice without even asking me if I wanted some. "All the fucking time. He's got some weird issue, and since I might know his dick more than my own, I don't really care."

I raise my eyebrows.

He chuckles before turning to the fridge and pulling out eggs. "I've known the guy forever. You know, locker room and stuff." He shrugs.

The toilet flushes and the water runs, signaling Jax is at least washing his hands again.

Knox washes his own hands then cracks some eggs into a bowl. "Do you like omelets?"

Jax walks by Knox, pulls coffee out of the freezer, and puts it in the coffeemaker. I watch in awe as they maneuver around like an actual couple, weaving and pausing around one another. Knox fills the pot of water and hands it back to Jax, who then takes the egg carton and puts it back in the fridge while grabbing cut-up veggies for Knox.

"Are you sure you two aren't a couple?"

They stop what they're doing and look at me, then their visions shift to one another. They both crack up laughing.

"I wish," Jax says.

"Life would be a helluva lot easier," Knox says, and I admire his forearm flexing as he beats the eggs into a scramble. He lifts the bowl toward me. "So do you?"

"Do I what?" I ask.

"Like omelets," Jax fills in and sits next to me.

"Yeah, but I was just going to head out." I shift my weight to slide off the stool.

Jax puts his hand on my shoulder lightly, pushing me back down.

"Stay for breakfast at least," Knox says. His eyes are genuine and honest, and it would be hard to ever deny that look.

"Okay, but then I have to go."

"Where to?" Jax asks, resting his head in his palm. "I thought you were homeless."

Knox keeps his side toward me, but I feel his stare from the corner of his eyes.

"Yeah, but I have friends."

"Friends you didn't have last night?" Jax asks.

When I'm about to wipe my hands of this and say forget it, I'm out of here, their apartment door opens, and the guy Knox was with all those years ago walks in.

"What the hell? You're trying to get Rian to be your fake girlfriend?" He leans his shoulder on the fridge, looking at Knox.

Knox glances at me, and a sour feeling coats my stomach. I don't know why.

"And the plot thickens." Jax sips his coffee, his eyebrows at his hairline.

"We'll talk about this later." Knox flips the omelet. His skills in the kitchen are impressive.

"Why?" Dylan asks.

"Because we have company," Jax interrupts.

Dylan's gazes shoot to us. His eyes narrow slightly, then he points. "I remember you."

"Kamea." Jax puts his arm around my shoulders. "She's staying with us for a while."

Dylan glances at Knox, but he continues to concentrate on the omelet and says nothing about me staying.

On one hand, staying here would be nice—I don't really have another option. On the other, I don't really know much about these men.

Knox lifts the pan and slides an omelet onto a plate, which he places in front of me. "Ketchup or hot sauce?"

I shake my head and accept the fork he hands me a second after he digs it out of a drawer.

"Are you with him?" Dylan asks me, pointing at Jax. "Because you know I have to tell Frankie if you slept with someone and ended the bet."

I unwind myself from Jax's arm that's still slung over me.

Jax laughs. "Hell no. She's Knox's."

"No!" Knox and I yell at the same time.

I guess that answers that.

Dylan chuckles, and he and Jax share some sort of look behind Knox's back. "Let me fill you in. Kamea here bailed out Leilani. Remember the girl—"

Jax can't finish his sentence before Dylan snaps his fingers and points. "That's where I know you from."

I nod. Although he looks slightly older and more confident in his own skin, Dylan looks exactly the same.

"Anyway… she bailed out Leilani and now she can't find her, but between getting out of jail and running away, Leilani got Kamea kicked out of her apartment. But our good buddy over here found her last night under an overpass and decided to play knight in shining armor like always. He dropped her off here last night and the rest is history, right?" Jax looks at me.

I nod, forking my omelet.

"Now you're going to live here?" Dylan asks, pouring himself a cup of coffee.

"No. I'm leaving after the omelet, which is delicious, by the way."

Knox smiles at my compliment.

Jax waves in front of my face. "Why leave? I thought we had a good thing going on here?"

I have no idea why Jax is so hell-bent on me staying here. He doesn't seem like someone who would want a girl ruining his game.

Instead, I say, "You don't even know me. And I don't know you."

"We know you're a nice friend who bails people out. We've all bailed each other out a time or two, whether it be at a police station or in life's circumstances," Dylan says. "I can swear by both these guys. You'd be safe here."

"Likely story coming from their friend." I raise an eyebrow.

Knox prepares another omelet and serves it to Jax. Before grabbing more eggs, Knox asks Dylan if he wants one.

"Give me a Bible," Dylan says. "Or the girls can vouch for them."

I finish chewing and decide to rip off the Band-Aid. "Why on Earth would you be so gung ho for me to stay? I could steal all your stuff in the middle of the night or something."

Jax looks me up and down before his eyes shift to Knox, who snickers, and Dylan, who outright laughs. "Yeah, I doubt that."

"What?" I glance down at myself. I'm wearing jeans and a sweatshirt.

"You got that sweet look going on." Dylan sips his coffee.

I frown and fork off another bite of omelet.

"Believe it or not, it's a compliment." Knox refills my orange juice.

"Yeah, my girl is even sweeter, so there you go," Dylan says.

Knox rolls his eyes, but I'm the only one who catches it. I think Jax might be hoovering his omelet.

"Which brings up my reason for coming over. Why are you trying to date my girlfriend?" Dylan asks Knox, who hands him his omelet, leaving himself last.

Again, just like when Dylan barged in, Knox side glances at me.

"I can go and leave you guys to talk," I say before wiping my mouth.

"That's okay," Knox says, beating the eggs for his omelet. "Leilani getting arrested is messing with my ability to get the detective position. Cap wants me to bring a date to show the big guys that I'm over my felon of an ex-girlfriend."

"Is she actually a felon?" I ask, but Knox shakes his head.

"So you picked my girl?" Dylan shoves some of the omelet in his mouth.

"Like you said, she's the sweetest." Knox eyes the eggs sizzling in the pan.

"True. I find myself jealous but complimented at the same time. She is the best, so of course if you have to bring a fake date, you'd choose her." Dylan smiles and winks at me.

Jax pushes his empty plate away from him. "Take Kamea."

"What?" I ask at the same time Knox's head whips around and he gives his friend a death glare.

"You're second sweetest next to Rian, from what we gather, and you're more Knox's type than Rian is anyway."

"Because she looks like Leilani?" Dylan asks.

"She looks nothing like Leilani," Knox says, and there's a bite in his tone that makes Dylan's head rear back.

Dylan rises from his chair. "I'm taking my omelet to go."

I wipe my mouth again and put my napkin on my plate. "No, I should go. Thanks for the omelet and for letting me stay last night. I'll just go grab my things."

None of them say anything. Jax's gaze is steady on Knox while Dylan eats his omelet.

Leaving the breakfast bar, I go to the room that was supposed to be mine for the night and pull my bags together. The horrible thing is, I have no idea where I'm going after I leave here. For a moment, the weight of my situation bears down on me and I almost collapse onto the bed.

But I have to suck this up and find my new path. I could go back to North Carolina, but that would only cause problems. I could ask my brother for money, but he's strapped for cash with his three kids. My parents aren't really an option since they haven't been in my life since I left home.

I pull out my cell phone and dial Leilani one more time with the hope that she answers. It goes straight to voicemail, so I hang up. *Just get out of here and you'll have a clearer head.*

I wheel my suitcase toward the bedroom door, only for Knox to walk in and shut the door.

"We need to talk," he says.

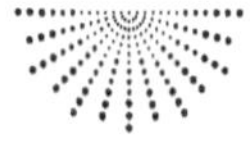

CHAPTER EIGHT

Knox

I ignore the murmurs from two of my best friends as I shut Seth's old bedroom door.

"Let's talk, okay?" I sit in the chair in the corner. The one that used to hold all of Seth's dirty clothes. The one that Evan said will not be going to their apartment—ever. The one Seth tried to sneak in only for Evan to return it when he went to work out.

Her hands rest on the handle of her suitcase, her gaze skittering to the door. Just when I think she's about to bolt, she sits on the edge of the bed, right next to her luggage. "Knox, you've done—"

I hold up my hand because I know she's going to say that she's fine and perfect, but we both know she isn't. Leilani left her high and dry with no money and no roof over her head. I don't know much about Kamea's friend or family situation, but the fact that she was sleeping under an overpass says there aren't any in the picture. At least not locally.

"Just stay. It's fine," I say. "Honestly. Jax doesn't care, and as long as you don't mind seeing him take a piss every morning, then it's all good. I promise you're safe here. And if you have any concerns, I have three women on this floor who could vouch for us."

Her shoulders lose some of their tension. "I don't feel unsafe."

"Regardless, Jax and I understand. You don't know us and here we are offering you a place to stay, but…" I glance at the door before I divulge my best friend's secrets to Kamea. "We come from a bad area of the city and we're used to looking out for people. And neither one of us would feel comfortable letting you walk out that door with no place to go. Think of it as a pay-it-forward when you get on your feet kinda thing." I shake my head. "But don't allow some strange guy to move in with you."

She giggles and shakes her head so that a few strands of dark hair fall from her ponytail. How could Dylan think she looks like Leilani? All that's similar is the dark hair and bronze skin tone. Kamea has a soft curve where Leilani had hard edges. Her smile is warm and caring, whereas Leilani hardly smiled and barely laughed.

"Are you sure? I mean, I literally have no money. I was supposed to do this bulk order of T-shirts that I sell, and I used the money to bail out Leilani. Without her appearing in court, I'm out the money."

"I have a few places we can try to find her. To get your money."

Her eyes widen in amazement that I would offer my well of knowledge when it comes to Leilani. "You'd do that?"

"Sure. I mean, I can't do it on duty, I have to be in regular clothes, but she had certain places she'd go around here.

Maybe we'll get lucky." I'd bet all the money in my bank account that she's long gone from Cliffton Heights by now, but I'm not telling that to Kamea because she'll lose hope.

Her excitement dims and she looks at her hands. "That's so nice, Knox, but this isn't your problem."

I shrug. She's right. Leilani isn't my problem anymore, but for some reason, that part of me that wants to fix her is alive and kicking inside me. I might not love Leilani anymore, but she has to stop doing this to people. "I know, but I can offer help, so I'm doing it."

"Why?"

Where did she and Leilani grow up that no one looked out for others?

"It's just the way I was raised." I stand before she delves into my upbringing too much. "Let me grab some sleep, then I have tonight off. We can stop by one of her haunts this evening."

She nods and I walk toward the door.

"Knox," she says, and I turn to face her. She's looking at her hands, twisting her fingers. "That party. If you need a date, I'd be happy to repay the favor and go with you."

I open my mouth, but nothing comes out at first.

"I mean only as a fake date obviously. I wasn't suggesting that—"

"I'd love that," I answer because I would. But I'm not digging into the reasons why at the moment. But since all my female friends are unavailable that weekend and I can't imagine allowing Patrice to be in charge of who attends on my arm, this works.

"Okay. Great."

"It's next Friday. It's casual, but maybe wear a dress. I'll ask Patrice." *Damn, Whelan, you're about as smooth as a jar of nuts.*

"Sounds great."

I walk out of the bedroom to find Dylan and Jax playing Xbox. Both glance up but go back to concentrating on their game.

"I'm headed to bed," I say. "Keep it down."

"So?" Jax asks, his thumbs moving a million miles an hour on the controller.

"She's staying and I'm going to help her find Leilani."

"What?" Dylan asks.

"You're dead," Jax says.

Dylan doesn't care apparently. He drops the controller. "I think that's a shit idea."

"Relax, it's just finding her for Kamea. I'm cool."

His eyes silently judge if I am actually good with it.

"And she's going to go with me to the party, so…"

Dylan laughs and sinks farther into his chair. "Oh, I gotcha."

"It's a favor swap, that's all."

Jax looks at Dylan, then shoots me a look to say "whatever" before his attention shoots back to the television. "Boring, if you ask me. Favor swaps should only involve sexual fantasies."

"Shit, I'm using that on Rian." Dylan pulls out his phone and texts something to presumably Rian.

"Doesn't work on girlfriends, dumbass." Jax's body leans to the side and he presses the buttons so feverishly, you'd think his life depends on whether he wins.

"You don't know Rian."

I open my bedroom door. "I'm going to bed now."

"Thanks for the omelets, bro. Sleep tight. Are you sure you don't want Kamea to tuck you in?" Jax mimics a sweet mother's voice.

"I wasn't the one on the couch with her this morning."

Jax's thumbs stop moving and his gaze moves to me. "She's all yours. The question is, do you want her?"

I let out an exasperated sigh. She's right in the next fucking room and can probably hear him. "I'm going to bed."

"Fuck me," Dylan says, glaring at his phone.

"She denied you, right?" Jax says.

Dylan say, "Yeah. What the hell?"

"I told you favor swaps don't work on girlfriends."

"The hell they don't. I'm going to Sweet Infusion."

The apartment door shuts as I shut my bedroom door. I strip down to my boxers, crawl into bed, and pass out the minute my head hits the sheets. I'm a little too eager for evening to come because I'll be spending more time with Kamea.

CHAPTER NINE

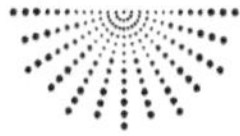

Kamea

Knox in uniform is intimidating, but sexy as hell. Out of a uniform, in jeans and a dark Henley with a leather jacket thrown over top, he's the same man who had my stomach stirring with butterflies all those years ago.

Jax is at work when Knox steps out of his bedroom, the room quickly filling with the intoxicating scent of a just-showered Knox. Thank goodness he doesn't wear cologne. I've never been a fan.

"Do you ride?" he asks, twirling keys around his finger while his gaze falls down my body.

I allow him to examine me because he knows where we're going and whether what I'm wearing is appropriate. I assume it is, since I look a lot like him in my jeans and one of my T-shirts that shows off that I'm a vegetarian. "The train?"

He chuckles and shakes his head. "Motorcycle?"

"Oh. I have before, but it's almost winter." Is he crazy?

"Streets are fine. All the leaves have been cleaned up by now. I spend most of my days locked in the car, so I ride until the snow flies. Do you have a warmer jacket?" Knox has this way of coming off as shy sometimes, which is endearing since he's a badass cop.

"Um. Not anything like what you're wearing."

He holds up his hand. "Hold on a second."

I stand in his apartment as he exits, leaving the door open, and knocks on the door across the hall. A tall blonde answers, and they converse for a moment before she glances around him and smiles at me. She raises her hand and disappears. Knox never turns back toward me. How did I ever get into an uncomfortable situation like this?

She returns with a leather jacket and holds it out for Knox. He takes it and turns back toward me, missing that the blonde follows him.

"Hi, I'm Rian," she says.

Dylan's girlfriend. The one Knox wanted to take to the retirement party. Interesting.

I shake her hand. "Kamea."

"I love your hair." She gestures toward my curls.

I decided to do ringlets instead of my usual straightening routine. Not that this is a date or anything. The ringlets have already turned more into waves now because my hair holds curls as well as hay would. "Thanks."

"Rian's going to loan you her jacket." Knox holds it out for me.

I reach out, but Rian grabs the jacket first and tosses it back to Knox. "Try that again."

His dark eyebrows scrunch, but he holds it out for me to slide my arms into.

"Dylan bought me this a few months ago," Rian says. "It's

heated by a little battery pack inside. I already turned it on for you, so you won't get too cold."

The jacket is a perfect fit and I'm immediately in love.

"There you go. Now you're a badass bitch." Rian giggles at her own joke. "At least that's what I always feel like when I wear it. Like I'm in a Halloween costume because it's totally not me."

"Thanks for letting me borrow it," I say.

Her hand runs down my arm. "Any time. You know, all the girls get together on Wednesday nights to watch *Sex in the City* reruns. Have you seen it?"

"Maybe a few late at night."

She claps. "Then come. I'll stop by and get you. Usually around seven or so. It's at Blanca's this Wednesday and she lives just down the hall."

"Don't force her," Knox murmurs.

I wonder if he'd prefer that I didn't associate with his friends.

"Did I put a pillowcase over her head and drag her out of here? I'm asking."

Knox blows out a breath. It's clear he'd rather not have me go, but Rian doesn't seem like the type to accept the answer no.

I say, "I'll think about it."

"Okay. I promise we're all nice. No mean girls or anything."

"So you guys don't wear pink on Wednesdays?"

Rian laughs and points at me, fixing her gaze on Knox. "I like her. A lot."

Knox's eyebrows bunch again. I'm sure he's never seen the movie *Mean Girls*. If he did, I'm sure he didn't memorize the lines. "Bye, Rian."

Rian walks backward. "Where are you guys going?"

Knox follows her until she's outside the apartment door. "You wouldn't know it."

"Okay, but we'll be at Ink Envy later if you guys want to hang out."

"We won't." He waves and she pretends to pout, lingering by her door. Knox turns toward me. "Ready?"

I grab my purse on the way over to him. He waits for me before shutting the apartment door and locking it.

"Oh, I forgot." He digs his hand into his pocket and retrieves a key on a keychain with a big K in pink rhinestones. "Here's your key."

"Thanks."

"Yeah, the selection of keychains sucked, and I knew if I didn't put one on it, I'd lose it."

"Ahh," Rian says, but when Knox and I look over our shoulders, she covers her mouth with her hand and waves off an apology for eavesdropping.

"Bye, Rian," Knox says.

"Bye you two. Have a great night." She waves and gives a thumbs-up as if this is a date.

Rian's definitely the romantic of the group, and I see why Knox would want to bring her as a fake girlfriend. She's got that innocent girl-next-door thing going.

Knox doesn't say anything but presses the elevator button. The entire situation feels like when you go on a date and your parents are watching from the porch until you're driving away.

The elevator doors shut. Knox's scent from the apartment lingers here now too. Thankfully it's only a few short floors before the doors open and he motions for me to exit first. He's such a gentleman. I want to ask him what happened with him and Leilani, but I have to remember it's none of my business.

Outside the apartment, by the curb, are three motorcycles.

"Middle one is mine," he says. "That's Jax's, and that's Dylan's."

"All three of you ride?"

He nods. "We all learned at the same time. Got our licenses the same day. A long time ago."

He takes the helmets off the bike and helps me with mine first. It feels kind of like I'm a bobblehead. Then he puts on his own and straddles the bike.

He glances at me then at the back of the bike. "Just hold on to me. I'll go slow at first. Lean into the turns, not away. I promise you'll be fine."

I climb on behind him, but I'm trying to keep my distance.

He laughs. "You need to move closer to me."

I inch up a little and lightly wrap my arms around his waist.

He tugs me and my ass slides along the leather. "Closer."

He situates me so that my crotch is right up against his ass and my hands are locked around his middle. His leather jacket is soft, and I can't help but wonder if Leilani was ever in this position. Then I mentally reprimand myself because of course she was. But she was probably able to inch her fingers up under the hem of his leather jacket and feel his abs.

"Good?" he asks.

I nod.

He starts the bike and moves out of the spot by walking his bike backward. I startle as he accelerates forward, but I'm surprised by how much I trust him. After a few turns, I really get the hang of being a passenger on a motorcycle, and I'm just starting to enjoy it when we pull up outside a house I don't recognize.

Kɴᴏx ᴛᴇʟʟs me to hang out by the bike while he climbs the broken cement steps up to a house I can't believe Leilani would hang out at. Two shutters with chipped paint hang cockeyed. The front door has a giant wooden plank over where it looks like glass broke. Beer bottles and liquor bottles line the railings of the covered porch.

I glance around the neighborhood. Most of the houses aren't in the best shape and are in need of a little tender loving care, but none of them look like they need to be demolished like this one.

Knox knocks and a woman wearing lingerie opens the door. *What the hell happened to you, Leilani?*

I'm not sure what she says, but a guy comes to the door, glancing at me and back at Knox.

Do these people know that Knox is a police officer? The way he stands on the porch with his legs spread wide and both arms crossed gives the persona of someone you don't want to mess with. The man is talking to Knox, but his gaze keeps straying to me. If I have to hear one more time that I look like Leilani, I might throw up.

Knox shakes the guy's hand, and the man hangs around the door while Knox walks down the stairs.

"Not here," Knox says, climbing back on. "We're headed to a bar now."

"Who is that? Is this a drug house?"

Knox laughs. "When was the last time you talked to Leilani before she called wanting bail money?"

I get the feeling maybe I don't know Leilani very well at all anymore.

Five minutes later, we're at a bar with a bunch of motorcycles parked outside. Most of the people wear leather, and even though it's late fall, most of the people are hanging out around their bikes rather than inside. My eyes scour the area. I had no idea Leilani hung out with motorcycle peeps, but I guess if Knox rides, maybe they're his friends.

"What's up, Five-O?" a guy with a woman on either side of him says to Knox. He blinks a few times, noticing me at Knox's side. "You're back?"

Knox blows out an annoyed sigh. "She's not Leilani, but we're looking for her. Have you seen her?"

"No."

Knox looks at me and nods toward the bar. "Let's get a drink while we're here."

"Okay."

The guy puts his leg out in front of me, stopping me. "Are you her sister?"

"No. We're just both Polynesian. I'm guessing all you see is our skin color?" I don't keep the bitterness from my voice.

His gaze skates over my body with a creepy smirk, and I inwardly shiver from whatever he's thinking. He says, "I guess Five-O does have a type."

Knox kicks the man's foot out of the way and grabs my hand. "I think you have your hands full, don't you, Noose?" He nods at the women by Noose's sides.

"Always room for one more." A girl dangles a cherry in front of him and he tips his head back, plucking it off the stem, his eyes on me the entire time he chews. "Let me know if Five-O doesn't treat you right."

Knox tugs a little harder and I catch up before he climbs the stairs. The bar is dark and dingy and there're more bikers throughout. Finding a table by a dartboard, Knox puts me so my back is to the door and he faces it. He raises his hand, and as though we're the only people in the place, a waitress comes over immediately.

"What do you want?" he asks me.

"Um… a beer?"

"Beer?" Knox asks.

I think I'll look weird if I order wine or some girly drink. Part of me thinks I should ask for whiskey neat.

Knox holds up two fingers. "Two Modelos."

"So Leilani hangs out here?" I scour the room, not understanding my friend at all. I thought she was all about righteous causes and saving the world.

"Yeah, there's something you need to know about your friend." Knox almost always looks serious, but right now, there's a tortured look on his face.

I try to prepare myself for whatever he has to tell me since it would appear he knows her way better than I do. Maybe way better than I ever did.

CHAPTER TEN

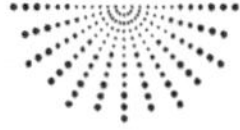

Knox

Kamea looks so out of place in this bar. It's not really my scene either, but Leilani liked the image of biker chick for a while, so I humored her. Pretty soon she had us joining a dart team here. That's how I met Noose.

As I sit across from Kamea, I'm not sure how to explain to her that her friend isn't always about the causes. Leilani duped me into thinking the same thing, but truth is, she's a trend chaser. Willing to get involved in anything she thinks makes herself seem cool, which is probably why I always thought I could save her. Make her realize her worth as a person and be who she is, not who she thinks others want her to be.

"What do you know about Leilani?" I ask, trying to figure out where I need to start.

Kamea shrugs. "She's for animal rights, she eats vegan…"

I'm a little relieved that's all Kamea really knows because it means they weren't all that close. Which oddly makes the fact that I kind of wish this was a date and not a search mission easier for me to accept. Not that I'd date Kamea. She's still linked to Leilani.

"The first house we went to is Jeff and Katie's. Katie met Leilani when they worked at an animal shelter together. Jeff and Katie are potheads and probably dabble in more. When I couldn't find Leilani, I used to find her there, just chilling during the day. This bar? We stopped for the food on a Sunday afternoon, then she dragged me here every weekend I was off for two months straight because she wanted to do the various charity rides for causes. I think this new stunt with the paintball is just another cause she feels nothing for but wants to belong to."

The waitress comes over and sets down the two beers.

After she leaves, Kamea asks, "What are you saying?"

"I used to think she was leaving me to go do good in the world," I say. "Every time I was with her, she'd have some new charity or cause, whether it be animals or child abuse or whatever."

She sips her beer and it's clear from her pursed lips she's not a beer drinker. "I don't see why that's bad."

I sip my own beer. "It's not bad per se, but Leilani floats around this world finding groups of people fighting for some cause they truly believe in. She's not necessarily about the fight as much as she is about fitting in. It took me a long time to realize that."

"Are you sure you're not just jealous because she didn't pick you?"

Her comment has me drawing back. I wait a moment to compose my thoughts, something I learned on the force early on. I couldn't be that smart-mouth kid I was growing up.

"No, I'm not jealous. I'll be honest… I had wished things

were different with Leilani, but I'm over that now. She uses people. She infiltrates a group, usually finds a way to get to the top of the ladder, then when she's bored or she thinks someone has figured her out, she bolts. Moves on to something else or just disappears." I gulp down my beer, wishing I wasn't having a conversation about the woman who took my heart and tore it in two.

Kamea twirls her beer bottle back and forth. "I'm sorry she hurt you."

"This isn't about me." I slide out of my chair, digging cash out of my wallet.

"What are you doing?" she asks, her innocent doe eyes questioning.

"We're leaving. I was wrong. I can't help you find her. I want nothing more than to forget her. And though I am over her, you giving me that sappy look like my dog got ran over by a semi isn't working for me." I throw a twenty on the table, but she puts her hand over mine and squeezes.

"I'm sorry."

I slide my hand out from hers, mostly because it's giving me thoughts I shouldn't have about her. "Don't be. I'm just sick of no one believing me. Shit, I'm sure my friends think you're the one to help get me over Leilani, but why do people think I'm lying?"

"If you sit down, I think I can help you with that." Kamea shrugs and her eyes shift to the vacant chair across from her.

I huff and sit down. "What?"

"You accepted her back so many times from what I heard."

"Who told you that?"

She picks at the label of her beer. "Jax did."

"Motherfucker."

"In his defense, I think he assumed I knew because just like everyone thinks you aren't over Leilani, everyone thinks she and I are close because I paid for her bail. But we aren't. I knew you left the bar with her that night, and she told me a little bit here or there when she was around, but I had a hard time piecing it all together."

"Remind me to thank Jax."

"I'm glad he told me." She looks at me with a look I've gotten from a lot of women in my life. She was thinking maybe there was a chance with us. "I mean, if you had just dated her that one time..." She shakes her head. "Never mind. Anyway—"

"What were you going to say?"

She picks at the label again. "You're so strong, outwardly, and you seem to keep a lot inside. I think people assume that if you fell so hard for her, that'd be a hard thing to get over."

I sip my beer. "It was. I was a mess for a long time, but the longer I thought about our relationship, the more I realized she used me. In a weird way, I feel like she used me as her stability, a constant she could come to when her life grew so out of control she didn't know where to go."

"That's not a bad thing."

"It is when I wanted more. I was all in with her. I was willing to change careers for her." I huff and down the rest of my beer. "I was a fool."

She places my hand between hers. "I'm sorry you were hurt, and if you say you're over her, then I believe you."

Her touch is soft, and I like it a lot. "Thank you."

"And you don't have to help me. I doubt we're going to find her anyway. I have to figure this out on my own. And I shouldn't be staying at your place either. You and Jax are so nice to offer, but it's probably not a good idea."

I don't say anything because I'm not sure what's right. "And you don't have to go to the retirement party with me."

She doesn't look up. "I don't mind, and I owe you for last

night. But I'll start figuring something out with the other stuff."

"Kamea," I say. She looks up with an expression of surprise, and I think it's because I rarely call her by name. I actually haven't called her anything because I'm afraid to get too close to her. "Just stay at our place until you get your feet on the ground. We have the room and we don't need the money. Honestly, these two places were my top ideas for finding her. I'm worried you're never going to see that bail money again."

It's easy to see Kamea isn't the type to overstay her welcome. As soon as she can afford it, she'll leave. I'm more worried she'll leave before she can afford a place.

She sips her beer which I'm sure is still practically full. "I don't know."

I glance to my right then look back at her. "Wanna play for it?"

Her eyes follow my line of sight to the dartboard. "Play for what?"

"To see if you stay with us." I stand and take the darts off the board, then I place the three red ones in front of her. "Whoever scores higher, wins."

"I'm actually playing you to see if I get my way and can leave your apartment?"

I laugh when she puts it that way. "I guess so. What do you say?"

"Well." She gets up. I love that she's already game with hardly any convincing. "I should let you know that I've played before."

"Well, crap then. How about two out of three?"

"Perfect."

I put out my arm. "Ladies first."

She steps up to the line and throws the first dart, hitting the wall instead of the board. I chuckle behind her.

"I need to warm up, it's been a while," she says.

I toe the line of tape that's coming up from the dirty floor, aim my dart, and decide at the last minute to play a little game with her. I hit the board but not on any points.

She narrows her eyes slightly but steps up for her second turn. She shoots it and actually scores, a double twenty. She jumps, her eyes wide as though she can't believe it. "Whoa!"

"Why do I feel like I'm about to be hustled?"

She falls back down to her heels and puts on a serious face. "Why would you think that?"

I laugh. She's fucking adorable. Anyone who thinks she looks like Leilani is insane. Her personality is so different, and it's a nice change from any girl I've dated recently. "I don't know."

I step up and don't really try but still manage to score a triple three. Nothing that will keep me in the game.

"That means I'm winning right now, right?" She hops up to the line and leans forward with her dart poised at the board, suddenly a lot more invested.

"Yep."

I'm not even sure she hears me as she moves the dart forward and back a couple times. She eventually releases the dart, and my eyes remain on her until she beams. I check the board. The dart sticks to the seventeen.

"I hit one!" she says.

"You did." I can't fight the smile from my face. I kinda wish she was mine so I could kiss her right now.

"Okay, hotshot, let's go." She signals for me to take my turn.

I throw the dart and I'm happy when I land a double one.

Her eyes narrow as she figures out the math, then she jumps up and down. "I won, right? I won?"

I nod, and her hips sway from side to side as her head

bops. She's so happy and I am too, even though I lost on purpose. Which I never do.

Then she stops. "We have to play again?"

"Yeah."

"Okay, loser first." She's still happy when the waitress comes over. "Oh, I'll have…" She leans forward. "Do you have anything kind of girly?"

The waitress eyes me and smiles. "I'll bring you what I drink." She picks up the beer. "And you? Another?"

"Water." I nod and position my dart.

The second game, we end up almost tied, but she falls short on the last dart. She's so busy sipping her drink that the waitress gave her, I'm not sure she cares.

"Final game," I say.

She hops off the stool and shoves me lightly with her hand. "Loser first, so that's me."

I sip my water bottle and watch her get into position. She wiggles her ass and her lips purse. Fuck me. I'm fighting to live with this girl? I'm going to be walking around with a hard-on every damn day.

We near the end of the game and she's ahead of me. I could play this cool, but the arrogant guy in me wants to show off a little. I throw it and it lands on the bull's-eye.

"*Knox!*" she yells and points. "You got a bull's-eye!"

I look at her with a cheesy grin on my face. "I did, which means…"

Her eyes turn to slits and she pokes me in my chest. "Did you just hustle me?"

I raise my hands. "No."

"Hmm… I'm not sure I believe you, but you won, so I stay."

Relief falls over her face and shoulders. We've all been where she is, so I don't say anything.

We return the darts to the board and go back to our stools.

"Now tell me about this T-shirt business. Is that one?" I point at the shirt she's wearing.

She looks down at her T-shirt that reads "I Don't Eat My Friends" and has a picture of a cow, pig, and chicken on it. "It is."

"You ate eggs," I say, remembering the omelet.

"I eat eggs. It's just animals that are slaughtered that I don't eat."

"I have to warn you, Jax and I are big burger guys."

"Well, maybe I can introduce you two to some other options."

This is going to be a problem—I'm actually excited about what she's going to introduce me to. Excited to come home from work and have her there. Excited to be able to talk to her whenever I want. Why didn't I throw the dart game? She's going to mess up my life. But right now, I don't even care.

CHAPTER ELEVEN

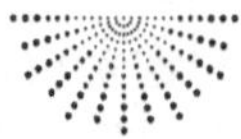

Kamea

 wake up the next morning and figure Knox must still be sleeping because he said he was off. I'm at the breakfast bar, sipping my coffee and designing new T-shirts—because I'm going to have to continue doing small orders until I can accumulate enough money for another bulk buy—when a door opens and my creative bubble is popped. I'm not sure whether it's Knox or Jax until the footsteps go to the bathroom, the door doesn't shut, and I hear someone peeing.

"You need to shut the door," I say when Jax comes out after washing his hands. At least he has on a white T-shirt and sweatpants instead of only his boxer briefs.

"Sorry, this one time I was jumped in a bathroom."

"Seriously?" I place my coffee down.

He shakes his head. "No. I'm just lazy." He grabs a mug

and fills it with the coffee I prepared this morning. "What are you doing?"

"Nothing much."

He peeks over my shoulder. "'Meat sucks'?" His eyebrows furrow. "Are you into girls?"

I laugh and roll my eyes. "No. I'm a vegetarian."

"Damn." He runs his hand through his hair. "I was thinking we hit the jackpot for a moment."

"Did you think if I was a lesbian, I'd have regular make-out sessions on the couch and you'd be able to beat off to us while we go down on one another?"

"I hoped, but you crushed that dream." He sips his coffee and waves his hand. "So explain then?"

"I'm a vegetarian, and I design T-shirts for vegetarians."

He nods. "Clever. What else do you have?" He grabs the edge of the computer and slides it to face him. "'Grass Fed.'" He scrolls. "'Bitch, Peas.'" He chuckles. "So this is the T-shirt thing, huh?" He pushes the computer back my way.

"Yeah."

"And she ruined it for you?"

I shrug. "I'll be fine eventually. I just have to work a little harder. I'll make more on the T-shirts when I can do a bulk order to get the cost per unit down, which was what I had planned for the money I spent on her bail. This way, I design them and someone else prints each one as it's ordered. There's a higher cost."

"So you can design any shirt and anyone can buy them?" He seems oddly interested.

"Yeah."

"If I wanted you to design one for my clients, could you?"

"Like for them to purchase?"

"I think I'll just give them out as gifts."

"Good business plan. What were you thinking?"

He looks up. "Let me think about it. Could you do it if I paid you for it?"

I stand to fill my coffee mug. "I don't want any charity."

"It's not charity. I'm going to profit from it."

"Profit?"

"Not money. Just pissing off a certain someone." For a moment his head is tipped back and he's smiling as though it's the best idea and he can't wait to pull off the prank.

Knox coming out of his bedroom interrupts us. He smiles at me, walking to the bathroom in only a pair of shorts. Damn, he's built. Abs ripple down his front and his ass makes me want to take a bite of it like an apple. The door shuts and I'm startled back to reality.

Jax laughs. "You've got some drool right there." He touches the corner of his mouth.

My face heats. "Shut up."

"You guys were out late last night. I expect a phone call from now on."

I roll my eyes and head back to my computer. Knox comes out of the bathroom and disappears into his bedroom for a second before coming back out to join us. When he passes me, I see he's put on a T-shirt—and I want to throw myself on the floor and have a fit like a toddler.

"Thanks for making the coffee," Knox says to me, pouring some into a mug then taking a sip.

"How do you know she made it? Maybe I did," Jax says.

"Because it tastes good." Knox sips from his mug again. "You coming or what?"

Jax groans. "Why don't you fools take a day off? It's Sunday."

"You don't have to come." Knox shrugs.

My head volleys between them as Jax stands. "Fucking hell. I'm going."

Knox smiles. "All the guys are on this workout regime.

Our non-single friends think they're getting guts. We're headed over to Adrian and Sierra's."

I hear a key in the door, and it opens, revealing a guy I haven't met yet.

Knox places his mug on the counter. "Give it to me," he says, holding out his hand.

"Don't you want me to have it in case of an emergency? What if our place is on fire? Or some crazy chick is here about to cut off your dick?" The dark-haired guy spots me in his peripheral and turns away from Knox. "Hey, I'm Seth and you are?" He sticks out his hand and I shake it.

"Seth, this is—"

"I didn't ask you," he says to Knox.

"Sorry," Knox says and fills a water bottle.

"Kamea," I say.

"Kamea? Is that Polynesian?"

"It is."

He shakes my hand the entire conversation.

Obviously, Seth knew Leilani based on the way he's looking me over. "Hmm…"

"She knows Leilani," Knox says.

Seth leans back on a stool. He's dressed in track pants and a sweatshirt. "Oh, I know. Rumors spread around here faster than TMZ."

"How did you find out?" Knox asks.

I'm actually happy Seth knows and I don't have to retell the entire story again.

"Group text." His head falls back. "That reminds me. I have something for you." He pulls a note out of his hoodie. "The girls were talking about you this morning."

That one sentence ignites a rupture so sour in my stomach, I fear I might throw up all over this counter.

He hands me the note. "This is from my girl, Evan." He winks.

"Seth just got a girlfriend. He's like an adolescent boy now who can't believe he can get laid whenever he wants."

I laugh at Knox as Seth flips him off.

I unfold the note and read the girly script.

WE'RE GOING to brunch today while the guys go workout. We'll be knocking on your door at ten to pick you up. Nothing fancy. ☺

KNOX IS STUDYING ME, and although I somehow feel close to him because I met him years ago, it's weird that his friends are so willing to welcome me. I could be gone tomorrow.

"The girls invited your girl to lunch." Seth smacks Knox's back.

Jax comes out of his bedroom.

Knox doesn't clarify that I'm not his girl, but I get the impression it's more because Seth doesn't seem like the type of guy who cares what Knox says. He'll say what he wants anyway.

The guys grab bags as Dylan and another guy, Ethan, come to the door and wait in the hallway, each of them waving hello to me.

Knox hangs back as the rest razz each other about how much weight they've gained. "You should go. You'll have fun." He glances over his shoulder at the guys and pulls his wallet out of his gym bag. "Do you need money?"

Humiliation must cast over my face. I feel as if I'm a child and he's my father. "No. I'm good, but thank you."

He puts his wallet away quickly, as though he'd like to forget it happened. "I didn't mean to offend you."

I shake my head because why wouldn't he think I don't have money? I don't. But I do have credit cards, and although my savings has taken a huge hit, I can pay for a brunch. "Thank you for the offer."

He nods and leaves, locking me in the apartment just as he did the first night.

I stare at the note.

Oh, what the hell. I haven't had brunch in a long time, plus as sad as I might sound, I wouldn't mind finding out more information about Knox and exactly how over Leilani he really is.

WHEN I OPEN the door at ten, three girls stand in the hallway. Rian, who I already met; Evan, with her long dark curly hair; and Blanca, who's so cute and petite she looks as if she could fit in my pocket.

After the introductions are over, we walk into the downtown part of Cliffton Heights, where the gazebo and park are nestled inside a rectangle full of shops and restaurants. Rian and Blanca walk ahead and discuss the guys and their ridiculous self-consciousness about gaining weight, while Evan stays back with me.

"So I heard something about you and T-shirts?"

I glance over, and Evan's warm smile makes me comfortable sharing with her. "Yeah, at first it was a quick way to make cash to supplement my income at the country club, but then people would send pictures of them wearing my T-shirts and their smiles just kind of sold me. So here I am."

Her grin is genuine. "That's awesome. I could moan about how long it took me to figure out what I love to do. I think I'm there now."

"What do you do?"

"She makes cream cheese." Rian glances back at us. "The best cream cheese in the world, and she sells it to bakeries even though if I could secure her all to myself, I would. But she's too pricey."

Evan rolls her eyes at Rian, but from the happiness splashed on Evan's face, she likes to hear the compliments. I don't blame her.

We reach the doors of The Backyard, which I know is well-known for their amazing patio during the warmer times of the year. I've never eaten here, but I hear people talk about it. We file in and shrug off our coats. A tall redhead stands and waves from a big booth in the corner.

"There's Sierra," Blanca says, and she leads the way for all of us to follow.

They each hug Sierra and say hello. She's dressed nicer than the rest of us in a pantsuit, while the rest of us are in leggings or jeans with sweaters. She's gorgeous, and I swear her skin actually glows. Then it dawns on me that she's Sierra Sanders from the news.

As the realization dawns on me, she looks at me. "And you're Kamea, right?"

"Yeah."

Sierra pulls me into a hug, and from the other girls' slack jaws and shared expressions, I figure this isn't something she usually does. "It's great to meet you. I'm Sierra."

I slide in next to Evan, and we all unwrap our silverware and place our napkins in our laps.

"Sierra is with Adrian, who is a prince," Blanca says.

"For now," Sierra corrects. "Once his brother is old enough, he'll abdicate the throne. His sister runs the country now."

I nod, remembering hearing about that years ago.

"I'd much rather hear the gossip with you guys," Sierra says as a round of mimosas are brought over by the waitress. "And I already ordered the first round." She raises her glass.

"To new friends." She winks at me. "And of course, our upcoming bride."

Blanca blushes, and we all clink our glasses and sip our drinks.

"You're getting married?" I ask Blanca.

"Yeah. Early next year."

"Oh, fun."

"You'll probably be there," Sierra says. When all the girls' heads whip in her direction, she shrugs. "Who else would Knox bring?"

No one says anything, but Sierra sips her mimosa and eyes me over the rim. I want to shift my gaze away, but I don't because that shows weakness.

"How close are you to Leilani?" Sierra asks.

And I'm quickly aware that maybe my invite to brunch wasn't about getting to know me, but more about how a set of protective sisters might interrogate the new girl in their brother's life.

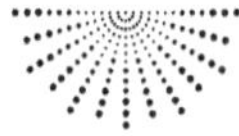

CHAPTER TWELVE

Knox

Adrian and Sierra live across the street from the Rooftop Apartments, where the rest of us live because we're not princes with a shitload of money. After working out in his building's top-notch gym, we head upstairs to their apartment, where Adrian makes us protein smoothies. The man has the self-control of a monk.

We sit around their table that overlooks the street and our apartment building.

"Let's talk about Knox's new girl." Leave it to Seth to bring up Kamea.

"Let's not." I tip back my water bottle, but all their eyes are on me when I lower my head back down.

"She's not Leilani, that's for sure," Jax says, standing and refilling his water bottle. "She's cool as fuck, and if you don't screw her, maybe I will." He winks.

Dylan sighs and rolls his eyes. Jax is one of my best

friends, and when he first returned to town after years away, he screwed with Dylan to force him to finally make a move on Rian. It turned out great since they're engaged and all now. But Jax better not be thinking of pulling the same shit with me.

"How about neither of us screw our new roommate?" I say. "Besides, you ready to lose that bet to Frankie yet?"

Jax narrows his eyes at me.

"So she's the new roommate, huh?" Ethan asks, journalistic curiosity in his eyes.

"She's got nowhere else to go," Jax says, sitting back down at the table.

"There are shelters and stuff. You don't have to be her saviors." Ethan eyes us as though he doesn't know how we'll take that piece of advice.

He's right. Kamea isn't our problem.

Dylan laughs and throws a balled-up napkin at Ethan. "Do you know Knox at all?"

Ethan shrugs. "I get the whole cop thing. But what about you, Jax?"

Our friends all know that the three of us grew up poor as fuck. Ethan didn't grow up with a silver spoon either. But Seth's family is middle class and they're close. And I'm not even gonna mention Adrian, who probably has safes and vaults full of valuables.

"Jax puts on a great act, but he has a savior complex too." Dylan smacks Jax on the back and picks up a smoothie from the counter as Adrian pours the last round.

"Don't go spreading rumors about me," Jax says to Dylan, but smiling at me. The three of us know more than we should about each other.

"The real question is, are Knox and Kamea sitting in a tree?" Seth sips out of his straw, his eyes on me.

I shake my head.

"Why?" he asks. "I saw the look you gave her earlier."

"She is hot," Dylan admits.

I'm surprised. I honestly thought the guy had been blind to any attractive female since he got together with Rian. I shrug, not having an answer.

"Come on. Why not?"

Seth knows me too well, which comes from being my roommate for so many years. He could tell from the minute I came out of my bedroom with a girl whether I was interested in her or not. Kamea is not only my type physically, but her personality is so opposite of any other woman I've dated that I'm intrigued. And Seth sees right through me.

"She's friends with Leilani," I say. "I picked Leilani over her at a bar ages ago. But the biggest reason why not is that she's down on her luck right now."

Silence falls over the table.

"Why does that matter?" Dylan finally asks.

I sip my smoothie to buy time. Our group of friends aren't really judgmental people. We might razz one another, but these guys generally know when humor is appropriate. Well, all of us but Seth probably.

So I say, "Because being the knight who saves or tries to save a woman hasn't really worked out well for me over the years. She'd come to resent me at some point just like…"

"Fucking A, she did a number on you." Jax leans back, shaking his head.

Jax wasn't really around for the whole Leilani thing except for the last part of the final time we were together. He saw the aftermath, and I think it scared him away even more from relationships. I was in bad shape.

"Sue me if I don't want to feel that shit again." I shrug.

"A date doesn't mean it will lead to heartbreak," Ethan says.

I hold up my hands. "As long as she's under our roof, I'm

not laying a hand on her. How much of a douchebag move would that be?"

"True," Seth says, which surprises me.

I kinda hoped someone would say it's cool to offer a girl a free apartment, then take her on a date without her feeling as though she had no choice but to say yes. But because my friends *are* stand-up guys, they all agree with Seth. And then it's case closed.

I find that I'm more disappointed than I would have thought. Kamea really does have to stay in the glass box I can't shatter—just like the fire alarms in our building.

"Let's go paintballing this afternoon. I need to let out some aggression," Jax says.

We all have the day off, including him and Dylan. They don't have to go into Ink Envy until tonight—if they have appointments.

"Let's call the girls now," Seth says.

While they handle that I walk out of the kitchen into their expansive family room showcasing floor-to-ceiling windows.

I stare at our apartments across the way. How did I get myself into this situation? Oh right, I put myself in it. I really need to learn to stop trying to give everyone a leg up in life. For some reason, I only end up hurt.

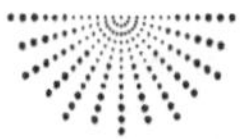

CHAPTER THIRTEEN

Kamea

"How well do you know Leilani?" Sierra asks.

All the girls shyly look in different directions. Blanca fixes her napkin. Rian situates her water glass and mimosa glass just so. Evan bites the side of her lip and looks at her phone in her purse.

"We used to be childhood friends. We grew up together. But over the years, we've gone our separate ways."

"But she called you to bail her out?" Sierra asks. I'm getting why she's a great investigative reporter.

"I did. She'd been staying at my place for two days before that."

She nods and places her mimosa down. "And now she's run off, not taking your calls?"

"Seems that way."

"I never really liked her. I'm sorry if you're still friends with her, but the way she was with Knox pissed me off," Sierra says.

Blanca and Rian nod.

"Dylan loathes her," Rian says. "Like, I think he might actually knock her out if he sees her again."

"Knox was miserable after she left the last time," Blanca adds.

My stomach flips. So I was right. Knox loved her.

Sierra glances in my direction, her expression softer than it was a moment ago. "But that's old news now. He's over her."

"Is he?" I find myself asking.

"Definitely." Evan touches my arm. "I'm newer to the group, but I never hear him talking about her. Seth's not a huge fan either. Says Knox was a different person when he was with her."

"Like how?" I ask.

They all groan and look at one another as though they're trying to figure out which one of them will answer me.

"Knox was always so protective around her. Like we were judging her, which we never were. Even when they came around, he'd barely talk to us, so concerned about her. And she would barely say a word." Sierra speaks first, which doesn't surprise me. She seems like she doesn't care what others think, and since I lack that backbone, I admire it.

Blanca says, "They just kept to themselves a lot. When we got together as a group, it would usually only be Knox. And he'd make up an excuse for her not being there."

I'm not about to say it, but I can see why Leilani might've been intimidated. All these women look as if they came from good homes and loving parents. Their hair is perfectly styled, and all their clothes look as though they came from trendy shops in the city. She most likely judged them—as she usually does—and set herself apart before they had the opportunity to.

"And the sex." Rian groans and Blanca elbows her. "I mean…"

The table quiets. I sip my mimosa rather than just sit there. My curiosity is piqued. When I was really close to Leilani, we were both virgins.

"Leilani is just comfortable with herself and so is Knox, so they didn't always find a private spot to… you know." Sierra waves her perfectly manicured hands as though it's no big deal.

I'm not surprised to hear that Leilani is comfortable in her body. She's always been that way. With good reason.

"But it's over now and here you are. We just wondered if you guys were close because you're living with Knox now. We don't really want her coming around and asking for her millionth chance with him," Sierra says and smiles.

But the vision of Knox and Leilani is still in my head. I give my head a shake, swallowing my mimosa. "Right now, she's skipped bail. Knox thought we might find her the other night, but we didn't. I'm just going to move forward and start saving again."

The waitress comes over and takes our orders, which I'm hoping will let this line of conversation die and we can start with something fresh once the waitress leaves.

"I heard you have a T-shirt business?" Sierra asks.

"I do." I nod.

"Can I see one?"

I pull out my phone and pass it over. Blanca snatches it from my hand to get the first look. "If anyone can help you sell some of those, Sierra can. She has her own fan base, plus everyone who follows her and Adrian." Blanca passes my phone to Sierra.

Sierra smiles. "I love these. I'm not a vegetarian, but

they're so funny. Look at these." She passes my phone to Evan.

Each girl takes an opportunity to scour through my store.

"I'm buying this one," Blanca says.

"The color mixes are gorgeous," Rian says.

"Where do you come up with your ideas?" Evan asks.

I tell them how I got started, and they all share their own stories, which somehow surprises me. I'd gotten the impression they all came out of the womb ready to conquer the world and be lady bosses. But even Sierra talks about the challenges of being with Adrian and the expectations that go along with it. Everyone has their individual struggles. There's something freeing knowing that.

"Don't feel bad about taking Knox and Jax up on their offer to stay with them. If it wasn't for Seth, I'd still be in my parents' garage. These are great and you're going to make it big one day." Evan's soft smile is genuine, and I appreciate it more than I could convey.

By the time we get to the mini desserts we all agreed to share, Sierra taps her glass with her knife. "Okay, brunch is almost over, so I have to ask the one question we all want to know."

Her gaze zeroes in on me, and I can guess the question before she asks. "Do you like Officer Whelan, Kamea?"

The other three girls turn toward me, waiting for an answer.

I blow out a breath. "I did at one point. And I won't deny he's hot, but he pushed me aside for Leilani years ago, so that's kind of a turn-off. I'm going to say that no, I don't."

"Uh…" Rian says.

"What?" Blanca says and looks at me. "Rian always has the gossip. Dylan is a huge sharer."

Rian giggles and holds up her hands. "He does tell me a

lot, but I don't know much about this situation. But I see it in Knox."

"See what?" I chuckle.

"The way his eyes follow you. It could be that he's just worried about you. That would fit Knox. He can be really private, so I don't know for sure. But personally, I bet he's kicking himself now because you are perfect for him."

I shake my head, not wanting to hear it. Even if I like that she thinks that.

"You never know what the future holds. This chick is marrying my ex-boyfriend." Sierra thumbs to Blanca and laughs.

Blanca covers her face with her napkin. "I thought we were over that."

"We are." Sierra lowers the napkin. "But sometimes you find the right person in the worst situation. I mean, Ethan didn't want to fall in love with my best friend and Blanca didn't want to fall in love with my ex, but it happened. Sometimes things like that aren't in your control." I say nothing, and Sierra takes it as a cue to continue. "I'm just saying I know when Knox made that decision years ago, it must have hurt you. But I'm sure neither of you are the people you were back then. You probably want different things now. Plus, how do you know it wasn't Leilani trying her hardest to get Knox that night?"

True. I can't deny Sierra could be right.

As we finish our mimosas and dessert, the conversation detours to Blanca's wedding and I relax a little more. I talk a good game, but even I know that if he tried, Knox could win me over faster than he can slap a set of cuffs on a suspect. And that scares the crap out of me.

CHAPTER FOURTEEN

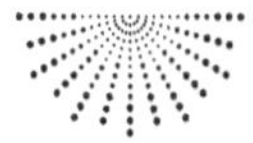

Knox

I wake up in the middle of the afternoon, unable to go back to sleep. I'm in the kitchen, getting a drink, when the front door opens and Kamea walks in with arms loaded with colored bags. I walk over to help her as she leans so far forward, I fear she might face-plant on the floor.

I take a few bags from her and she looks up, but she's eye to eye with my dick. My morning wood, to be exact.

Fuck, I forgot about that. I'm still getting used to having a woman living with us. It's like a Christmas morning surprise every time I walk out of my room and see Kamea.

"So sorry." She stands erect and turns her head as far from me as she can.

"No, I should be sorry." I set the bags I took from her on the counter before heading back into my room to put on a pair of sweatpants and a T-shirt rather than stay in my

90

boxers. When I emerge, she's busy putting away the groceries. "Sorry about that."

"It's okay. It's your apartment. You can walk around however you want." She puts the organic milk in the fridge, along with her tofu. She's already replaced the eggs since we ran out yesterday.

"Then feel free to walk around in your bra and under-wear," I joke. If she does that, my morning wood is gonna look more like granite.

She giggles. "Yeah, right."

I unpack the groceries, checking out what this woman eats. Not much that I would consume, that's for sure.

"You don't have to help. I got this." She takes a cereal box out of my hands.

"It's okay. I don't have much else to do. I can't sleep."

"I have no idea how you handle that overnight shift. I'd be parking my car in an alley and falling asleep during it." She folds up her reusable grocery bags and puts them all in the biggest one.

"I'm not really used to it yet. We switch our shifts every quarter, and this is my least favorite."

Her eyes meet mine for the first time. "I can see that."

She heads to her room, but I need to tell her something, so I turn around. "I might have one more place we can look for Leilani. Her court date is coming up quick, so if you're cool with it, we can do it this weekend?"

"You know what, it's fine. I'm fine. If she comes back, great. If she doesn't, then I'll manage."

I tilt my head, not understanding why she'd be okay losing out on the money.

"But do you think you could come to my old apartment in Peekskil and help me get some of my things from my the building manager's?"

"Do you want to go now?"

Her eyes light up. "Really?"

"Definitely." I might not be able to find Leilani for her, but I can help her get some of her stuff here so she's more comfortable. "I'm starved though. Mind heading to this pizza place I know of first?"

She glances at the clock. "Sure. Yeah, I have to make something for girls' night, but I have plenty of time."

"I'll just shower quick and then we'll go."

IT MIGHT BE the quickest shower of my life. When I emerge, she's sitting in front of our television with her laptop on her legs as usual. She really is a workaholic, and I'd offer to pay for that bulk order of shirts if I thought she'd accept them.

Jax walks in as I step out of the bathroom without a shirt. Have you ever put on a shirt in a steam-filled bathroom? It's not so I can watch Kamea do a double-take at my torso. But Jax whistles, and I shake my head.

"You two going out on a date?" Jax walks into his room and comes out with a book. "I forgot my sketchbook."

Kamea swivels around in the chair, her interest piqued.

I disappear into my room and grab a shirt and sweater since the weather is shitty. When I come back, she's sitting on the couch, her legs tucked under her, and Jax is telling her about some of the tattoo sketches in his book. Bragging about his Instagram following and how he's well-known in the tattoo world. Kamea eats it up, and I think back to the other day at Adrian's. I'm not sure Kamea would even entertain dating me if I wanted to date her. Jax might be more her type now.

"Ready?" I ask.

Jax shuts the book and stands. "Where are you two off to?"

"We're going to pick up my stuff from my old landlord's," Kamea says.

"But first we're stopping at Slices of Heaven."

Jax digs into his pocket for his wallet, as I knew he would. It's been a favorite of ours forever. "Two slices of sausage?"

I pocket the money. "It might not be hot by the time we get back."

"I'll eat it a week old, I don't care. You two have fun, but not too much fun." He winks, then he's out the door.

"This pizza place is that good, huh?"

I grab her jacket and hold it out for her. "You'll see."

We head down the elevator and out to my car, which I'll drive from now until spring. The weather is turning colder by the day. Kamea climbs into my beat-up Bronco that I bought for fifteen hundred dollars. The hinges whine when I shut the door.

She fastens her seat belt, and if she's at all fazed about the shit vehicle I just put her in, she doesn't show it. Usually if I'm dating, I'll get an Uber or give some excuse for why I can't drive. Women like the motorcycle, but the Bronco not so much.

"How long did you live in Peekskil?" I ask, pulling out of the parking spot.

"Two years," she answers.

"And you've never been to Slices of Heaven?"

"Nope. I'm curious where it is compared to my apartment. I'm kind of a homebody." Her voice is shy with a hint of embarrassment.

"What was your go-to takeout?" I ask to let her know I'm not a homebody, but I do enjoy time in.

"Well, there's this poke bowl place by my house. It was usually that or Chinese. Depends on my mood."

"Why do you love being home so much?"

She side-glances me. "Are you practicing for that detective position?"

I laugh. "Sorry, just trying to get to know you."

"I'm not a crowd person. But unfortunately, staying at home so much left me without a lot of friends. Without friends, it just kind of snowballed and I'd stay in more."

"You had Leilani," I say.

"Yeah, at one time, but I meant what I said. We haven't seen one another in a while. The last time I truly hung out with her was in high school."

"But that night we first met at the bar…"

God, that night has been haunting me lately, and I need to stop obsessing about it. It's done and over. Kamea obviously doesn't care or hold it against me. But regardless, it's about time I apologize for that. When she doesn't say anything, I figure now's the best time.

"I'm sorry about that night, by the way." I pull onto the highway and the wind sounds increase in the old truck.

"You have nothing to apologize for."

Lowering the volume on the radio, I wait until I think I have her attention—which is hard, since I'm driving. I should've waited to have this conversation until after we were done eating. Maybe I should hold off. I should look her in the eye when I apologize. So I turn the radio back up.

We drive the rest of the way in silence until we pull off the exit in Peekskil and she points out where she's from. "I live down that way."

Her former apartment isn't in the best area of Peekskil, not that there's a horrible part of the city.

"Yeah, Slices of Heaven is on the other side."

So we drive away from her apartment and head to the opposite side of Peekskil to the pizza place Jax and I found on a fall motorcycle ride years ago. Back when I was healing a shattered heart.

I park in the lot and she exits the truck before I can get there, which is fine because this isn't a date. This is just two roommates going to dinner. If only my eyes would stop straying to her ass. Kamea reads the sign on the front of the building.

"Are you telling me it's set up like a pizza buffet?" she asks, excitement in her tone.

"It is, and they serve beer. It's like a double win."

"If you like beer I guess."

"They have a great beer here from a local brewery. You have to give it a shot and see what you think."

She shrugs. "Okay. I can't believe I've never been here, and I was living so close." Her footsteps pick up speed.

I open the door of the small restaurant for her. It's brightly decorated in red and black and white. This was made for a college town. She reads the directions and grabs a tray, her smile still in place. Her whole aura right now is happiness. It's nice to see. We walk down the line, her taking two pieces, me taking three, and adding breadsticks and two beers.

A waitress sits us at a table for two in the back, thankfully away from the couple of families. Not that I mind kids, but I want to have a serious conversation with Kamea.

I pour our beers in the mugs they supplied as Kamea unwraps her silverware. I slide one over to her and motion for her to take a sip. "What do you think?"

She swallows and then looks over at me with a smile. "Actually that's pretty good."

I grin. "Told you. Anyway, as I was saying in the truck—"

She holds up her hand. "We don't have to have this conversation."

"I'd like to, if it's okay."

She stops arranging her pizza and sits back in her chair.

"We had a connection that night, right?"

Her eyes meet mine and she nods. "I thought so."

And there it is. I did hurt her all those years ago. "I was coming off a breakup. A girl from college I'd been dating. I wanted something just for the night. You're not—"

"Leilani. I know." She crosses her legs and tucks her hands under her thighs.

"No." I shake my head and scowl. "I meant to say you're not someone a guy wastes a one-night stand on."

She rolls her eyes. "Well, thanks."

"Damn, I'm messing this up." I push a hand through my hair and blow out a breath. "You're a take-home-to-mom kind of girl. The one you want to meet when you're ready to settle down."

"I guess a guy will finally approach me when I'm forty." She smiles though, and I'm hopeful she sees it as a compliment.

"It's a good thing. But I wanted to apologize because I was a young punk then. To flirt with you and take your friend home." I shake my head.

She shrugs and picks up her silverware. "It's okay. I'm kind of used to it when it comes to Leilani."

"What?" I draw back, shocked.

She waves her fork as though it's no big deal. "Everyone loves Leilani. She's a good time. I'm not surprised you did too."

The conversation dies as I realize something. Every girlfriend I've had has usually had a best friend who's the polar opposite. The outgoing one and the quiet one. The outgoing one who keeps the quiet one in their shadow.

"Tell me more about high school with you two, if you don't mind?"

Her facing going white, she drops her fork and it falls onto the floor. She doesn't immediately try to grab it. Then she snaps out of her daze and picks up the fork and puts in the dishwasher bins by the garbage. She returns to the table with fresh silverware, and I wait for her to say something.

"Not much to say, honestly."

I'm obviously missing a very big piece of the puzzle when it comes to Leilani and Kamea's relationship. Whatever went down between them, it went down in high school.

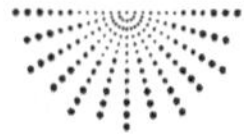

CHAPTER FIFTEEN

Kamea

I didn't live in a bad area, but it's not in the cared-for downtown part Peekskil.

The pizza would've been better if I hadn't been worried about Knox seeing right through me after he asked me about Leilani and high school. I appreciate his apology for the night we originally met, and it only confirms what I seem to have always known about Knox—he's a great guy. But he didn't say he's looking for a relationship now. Or even that he'd want one with me.

"Hey, Sally," I say when my former building manager answers the door in her going-out wear—spandex and black nylon tights. She might still think it's the eighties.

"How are you?" she asks, opening the door and eyeing Knox. "And who are you?"

"Oh, this is Knox."

"Her roommate." He holds out his hand, and she shakes it.

"Man, girly, you sure recovered quickly. Wish I had a roommate that looked like you." She eyes Knox from head to toe.

Pink colors Knox's cheeks, and he glances at his feet.

Yeah, I'm swooning right now with you, Sally.

Knox walks to the pile of my stuff in the corner of the room, ignoring Sally's flirting and my dreamy eyes. "This all yours?"

"Yeah."

He picks up my flat-screen television. The one I bought with my tips from the country club last Christmas. The rich do tip well around the holidays. Knox walks the TV out of the apartment while Sally sits at her vanity that she keeps in the family room because she can't be away from her soap opera channel.

"He's a cutie. How'd you hook up with him?" she asks, lowering one eyelid to put on purple eyeshadow.

"A friend of a friend. He's being nice and letting me stay with him. Figured I might as well get this stuff out of your way." I pick up a box, but Knox walks in and takes it out of my arms without a word.

"Well, your friend of a friend needs to become a friend with benefits. I just want to smack his ass."

Knox walks in as she says it, and he turns his attention to the floor until I pick up another box. He quickly grabs it from me.

"Let's not sexually harass him," I say.

Sally swivels around and I see a run in her nylons by her toes where she's painted it with red nail polish to stop the run. "I meant to tell you, I saw one of those idiots yesterday."

"Who?" I ask, collecting some of my stuff and condensing it into one container.

"One of the boys who got you kicked out."

"You did?" My eyes fly to the door, but Knox hasn't returned yet.

"Wanted to let you know that they're around. Maybe your friend is too."

Yeah, she probably is, but I honestly couldn't care less. I'm on my own island right now, and I'm happy that way. How long can I let the guilt from what happened in high school overtake my entire future?

"He was talking to some other idiot who lives in the building and he said they've been staying at a place in New York City."

"Who is they?" Knox walks in and I look at him. "What's going on?"

"Sally saw one of the guys who was with Leilani. Apparently, he said they're staying at a place in New York City."

He grimaces. "Yeah, I figured they'd all left Cliffton Heights for good."

"Cliffton Heights? Is that where you're staying?" Sally asks with disdain in her tone.

"That's where I live," Knox says. "I'm a police officer there."

"A cop? You're a cop? You don't look like any cop I've ever known." Sally stands up and slide into her red heels. "I'd be less surprised if you told me you strip on the weekends."

An image flashes in my head of Knox with a G-string on. Yeah, doesn't fit him at all.

Knox nods at the final box. "Is this it?"

I grab the floor lamp. "Yeah. I rented the apartment furnished."

Knox leaves, and Sally leans in. "Are you sharing a bed with him?"

"No!" I screech. "They had a buddy who just moved in with his girlfriend, so I have his old room."

"Jeez, you act like it would be a bad thing." She rolls her

eyes.

Knox comes in and shoots me a look that clearly states he's ready to go.

I try to hide my grin. "Thanks again, Sally. Have a great night out."

"Anytime, sweetie." She walks us to the door. "And if you have any older cop friends who look like you, give them my number," she says to Knox.

He nods, smiles, and holds out his hand to her. "Nice to meet you."

"Oh, we'll be seeing each other tonight in our dreams." Sally winks.

Knox's mouth opens before he shuts it. This cannot be his first time being flirted with by an older woman.

We leave Sally's and hop back in his Bronco. Which I love, mostly because it shows a side of Knox that I admire. The motorcycle is custom and decked out. He views this truck as a means to get him from point A to point B. He's not all about his image and what others might think, otherwise he would've upgraded the Bronco a long time ago.

Silence falls over the car ride as he pulls onto the highway to head back to Cliffton Heights. I hate the way I pushed off his conversation starter about high school, but I figured he was looking for more information about Leilani because he still loves her. I like Knox, and if nothing else, I would love a friendship with him. But in order to do that, I need to be willing to have a conversation about Leilani.

"So are you in that spot in your life again after Leilani?" I ask.

He scowls out the windshield. "What?"

"You know… Leilani obviously hurt you. Your friends say it destroyed you. So are you looking for a good-time girl or a long-term girl now? Especially since you were so serious with Leilani?"

"Remind me to thank my friends."

"I'm not trying to pry."

His chuckles bring life to the truck. "How about we both lay out the cards?"

"Cards?"

He nods. "I hate fishing for information. It makes the cop in me assume the worst. I do want to get to know you, and the reason I apologized earlier was because I want to get rid of this wall I feel like is between us."

Somehow, I refrain from putting my hand over my heart and swooning. "Why?"

"Why what?" he asks, putting on his turn signal to get off at Cliffton Heights exit.

"Why do you want to get to know me?"

He smiles in this shy way that makes him even more attractive. "Tell you what? Let's go to the apartment and we'll go up to the rooftop. Have the actual conversation we should have had already."

"You do know we're, like, two weeks out from Thanksgiving?"

"Don't worry. We'll grab blankets."

"Okay."

JUST AS HE SAID, while I was changing into warmer clothes and grabbing the blanket, he was making warm spiced apple ciders.

"Ready?" Knox asks.

I nod. My nervousness over having this conversation puts my fear of how cold it will be on the back burner.

He holds both cups of cider and I grab a blanket for him. "You know I'm too manly to actually use it, right?"

"It's okay, you don't have to be all macho in front of me."

"That's good to know." He grins and I swear to God my lady parts sigh.

He directs me up the stairs and out onto the roof, turning on lights that are strung across the roof.

"It's so pretty."

"Yeah, the girls seem to like it." He sets the mugs on the table, one across from the other.

I pass him a blanket. "Just in case."

"Ah." He tosses it onto a vacant chair, laughing.

I'm enjoying this side of Knox. We sit down and the chairs are chilly, to say the least, but even with the cold, I don't really want to go in. It's romantic out here with the hanging lights, snuggled in blankets and drinking apple cider. Romantic except that he's across the table from me and not next to me.

"Ladies first." He holds out his hand between us and sips his drink.

"I'm cool to go second." I sip my own, tightening my blanket around my legs.

"Okay then," he says, laughter bubbling up his throat. "Leilani crushed me. Bulldozer crush."

I wait to raise the white flag and call this over now. I want to know, but I don't want to hear about how much he loved her either. I refrain from saying anything.

"I honestly didn't understand why she couldn't stay. You know? Like wasn't I good enough and all that shit." He sips his cider again.

I should tell him why he's not enough to stay. That it's not him, it's her.

"Then after a few months, I figured out I was forcing her to be someone she wasn't. When my college girlfriend screwed me over, that night at the bar, I just wanted to forget. I didn't want to involve my heart in anything again. And for a while with Leilani, my heart wasn't invested.

Then… the next time she stayed longer, and I really fell for her. Wanted to protect her, but I'm not quite sure I ever really knew her."

"I think closeness scares her."

He nods. "Yeah. I got that, since she never shared anything with me. I never knew anything about her past. But to answer your question in the truck, no, I'm not the young idiot I was back then. Leilani hurt me, but I like to think there's someone out there who wouldn't mind me loving them. Who wouldn't see my love as suffocation or me trying to change them or force them to be something they're not."

"Definitely." I bury my head in my cup. "But are you sure you're over her?"

"Yes," he answers without hesitating, and our eyes lock for a moment. Is he trying to tell me something? But he diverts his gaze too quickly for me to be able to tell. "Now it's your turn."

I inhale a calming breath. "Well… um… Leilani and my families are close, as is most of the Polynesian community where we lived. But I'm not sure we would have been friends if we hadn't been next-door neighbors and had our parents not been such great friends. I mean, we're so different."

He nods. He doesn't have to mention them—I'm well aware of our many differences.

"I-in high…"

He sips his drink, and his gaze finds mine over the rim of his mug. Oh, screw it. What do I have to lose by being truthful?

"In high school, we were at a party and I was flirting with this guy. I ended up getting drunk and he took me upstairs. Leilani arrived right before the guy got what he wanted from me. His friends busted in and a huge fight started. Leilani got me out of there, but the boys bullied her afterward. Told her she was a cockblocker. Put things on her locker. It ended up a big mess. You know in high school where it feels like everything is a huge deal? You can't see that there's life outside of those walls?"

He nods, but that smile that's been a permanent fixture on his face is no longer there. He huffs and asks, "Would she have bailed you out of jail?"

"Truthfully, I hope I never go to jail. But if I did, I wouldn't be able to find her. That's the thing with her—she only comes around when she needs something. She came to me the night before we graduated and asked me to run away with her afterward. But I couldn't. I've always wondered if I had, would that have changed things?"

He stares at me until I look away. But he leans forward and takes my chin and directs my gaze back to him. "I'm going to tell you something you probably don't agree with, but being a cop, I see people like you all the time. Family members who feel they somehow failed their loved one and that's why they're screwed up. Leilani has to own her decisions. Maybe she needs therapy or whatever. But she has to be the one to seek that out. And you have to stop thinking it's solely that one event that made her like she is. Maybe she just never wanted to settle down."

He lowers his hand, but his eyes remain on me. I pick up my mug to avoid looking at him.

"You're a good person, Kamea. But you can't be everyone's savior, especially when they don't want to be saved."

I nod and lower my forehead to my covered knees. He's so right. I know he is. I've told myself that. My brother has told me. But every time Leilani reenters my life, all I see is the girl who sneaked in my window one night and looked so desperate to catch a bus out of town. And the disappointed look when I said I couldn't go with her.

Knox isn't the only one who has regrets where Leilani is concerned.

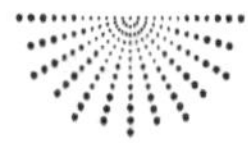

CHAPTER SIXTEEN

Knox

The next day, I'm at Ink Envy, and Frankie and Jax won't stop arguing about some customer Jax says she stole last night. Poor Dylan. If he wasn't so close to both of them, I think he'd fire one just to make his life easier.

The door opens and all the girls, including Kamea, come in. After our conversation on the roof things have been easier with us. I feel like we're becoming friends—although I can't stop wondering what it would be like if we were more. I meant it when I told the guys I never want her to feel as though she has to have sex with me just to have a place to stay.

Kamea lays a garment bag on the chair next to her.

"You got a dress for the retirement party?" I ask.

"I borrowed one from Sierra. She's got a nice collection of fancy stuff."

"And probably a whole other full closet in Sandsal. The girl is definitely lucky," Blanca says.

If Kamea was mine, I'd buy her a dress, but I'm fairly sure saying that would land on the creepy side.

"And she's coming over to Rian's before to have her makeup and hair done." Blanca points at me. "You'll pick her up there."

"Okay," I say.

"Those are their rules, but I can just meet you in the hallway or something," Kamea says, shaking her head as though the girls are being unreasonable.

I'm used to the girls being bossy. "No, I'd be happy to pick you up from Rian's."

"And my house," Dylan says from his tattoo station.

"I got some time. Want me to do a decent job on that fill-in?" Jax says.

I look back assuming he's talking to me, but Kamea stands. "Are you sure?"

He nods. "Yeah, you designed that T-shirt for me and didn't charge me for your time, so this is me paying you back. I had a customer, but they just canceled." He puts his chair up and Kamea slides onto it.

"Where's your tattoo?" I ask.

Frankie laughs. "We're all professional here, officer," she says, wiping a cloth down her client's ribcage.

"Just on my arm," Kamea says.

"Man, you spoke too fast. I was about to get his jealous side alive and kicking." Jax shoots me a cocky smirk.

I say nothing. The man knows me too well and sees that I might be into Kamea.

Jax prepares his workstation, washes his hands, and puts on gloves.

"What's this thing with shirts?" Blanca comes next to me,

situating herself so she can still have a conversation with all the artists.

Kamea opens her mouth, but Jax beats her to the answer. "Just something between us. You'll all find out eventually."

"Oh, I'm on the edge of my tattoo chair," Frankie says.

"You'll like them the most." He winks, and she rolls her eyes.

The bell on the door rings as Jolie, Frankie's daughter, walks in.

"Hey!" Blanca says, holding out her arms.

Jolie hugs Blanca right away. Her grandma lingers by the door but sits down since Frankie is still working.

"I'm almost done, baby. Sit with Knox and Blanca. How are things, Sandy?" Frankie asks Jolie's grandma, her ex's mother. Complicated situations seem to be the thing around here.

"Good. You know the shelter I help out at on Thanksgiving?"

"Yeah?"

Everyone's attention rests on Sandy while I can't stop watching Jax and Kamea. This is not good.

"Well, the guy who was supposed to play Santa on Thanksgiving just canceled. So now we're scrambling."

"Play Santa?" Jolie says, and the room quiets.

"We talked about this, Jolie. Santa has helpers," Frankie says.

Jolie's mouth falls open, and she looks at Blanca and me in disbelief.

"The big guy can't do it all by himself," Jax adds.

More stunned silence fills the room. Jax has a soft spot for Jolie, but he refuses to admit he has a soft spot for her mom too.

Jolie zeros in on me, walks over, and leans close. "Are you one of Santa's helpers?"

Blanca chokes on a laugh.

I try to act serious when I really want to ask the little girl if I look like an old fat man who eats cookies daily.

"Why would you ask that?" Sandy asks.

Jolie looks at her grandma and back at me. "He looks like a young Santa. Big, and he kind of has a beard."

"Big?" I ask.

Blanca laughs again.

"Does Santa's stomach look like this?" I lift my shirt and show off my six-pack.

"Put your shirt down. The girl was just asking. It's a compliment." Jax winks at Jolie.

I spot Kamea's heated stare on my stomach and a rush of electricity runs through my body. How could I ever be jealous of her and Jax when she only looks at me that way? I lower my shirt and Kamea turns her attention to Jax.

"Good thing the dress is long-sleeved," Blanca says.

"Oh, I didn't even think about that. I should have waited." Kamea looks at me.

I shrug. I don't really care. Plenty of my coworkers sport tattoos. "As long as you're comfortable."

A tugging on my pant leg turns my attention down. "Knox?" Jolie asks.

"Yeah?"

"Will you play Santa for my grandma's shelter?"

"I'm sorry, what?"

"I'm sure he would love to, Jolie," Jax says with a grin.

"Yeah, he loves to do stuff like that," Dylan shouts from his spot.

"Come on, guys," Frankie says and crooks her finger for Jolie to come to her. She leans forward and whispers something.

Blanca smacks me on the arm. "You're going to disappoint her."

Jolie comes back over to me, her bottom lip quivering and her eyes tearing up. *Oh shit, Frankie. Seriously? Come on.*

"I'm sorry, Knox," Jolie say quietly.

I look at Frankie and sigh. She shrugs and continues tattooing. Jax coughs out, "Grinch." Blanca hits me again.

"Okay, I'll do it," I say.

"Really?" Sandy asks, and I half wonder if I was set up.

Jolie jumps up and down, clapping. She runs over to Frankie, and they air high five.

"Got you," Frankie says.

I shake my head and ignore them. As though I could've really said no to Jolie.

"See, he's a good guy like that." Jax nods to me while his needle buzzes over Kamea's arm.

She smiles brightly at me as though she's just as enamored as little Jolie.

"I gotta go sleep before work," I mumble and walk out of the tattoo shop.

When I get to my apartment, I do what I've been doing almost every night. I beat off to visions of what I think Kamea looks like under her clothes, then I pass out like a baby until my alarm blares at nine.

"So you're bringing the waitress?" Patrice asks when we call in for our dinner break, walking into the sandwich shop we usually eat at since we started on the night shift.

"Kamea. Yes."

"Is that your type then? Polynesian?" She looks over her menu as though we've never been here before.

Sometimes I feel as if I'm in a relationship with Patrice. I mean, we spend so much time together. Especially on this overnight shift, where there are sometimes hours with nothing for us to do.

"No. It's a coincidence."

"You like her?"

"Who?"

She rolls her eyes. "The waitress."

"Kamea," I correct because it annoys me when Patrice refers to her as the waitress. It brings up that night, and although Kamea seems good with my apology, it's like a splinter I can't get out from under my skin.

"Yes, Kamea. Do you like her?"

We're interrupted by the waiter taking our order. Patrice gets the grilled chicken salad, and I get a burger with fries. Normally I eat leaner, but having Kamea in the house, I've been forced to try hummus and tofu this week. Time to reclaim my man card.

Once the waiter is gone, Patrice sips her water. "So we're starting fertility treatments. I'll apologize in advance if I'm a bear to deal with these coming weeks."

I'm thankful she's moved on to a new topic. "That's great."

"I might need you to give me a shot."

I choke on my drink. "What? No."

"Come on. I hate needles, and I can't have Nate wake up just to come give it to me."

"We can drive you to him," I say.

She tilts her head and gives me the same look my mom did when she didn't much care for what I said. "Seriously?"

"I'm a cop, not a doctor," I say, pulling out my cell phone to see if I missed anything. Although most of my friends are asleep. If I had a real girlfriend, I wonder if they'd send me a sexy message or just a quick good night. Would my shift drag on longer, waiting to return to them?

"You're kind of a romantic, huh?" Patrice interrupts my wandering mind.

Thank God because I don't need to be thinking about that.

"No." I tuck my phone away. "You've known me for three years. Have I given you the impression that I'm a romantic?" I raise an eyebrow.

"I saw you during your worst heartbreak. You want more than some chick in the bathroom stall, don't you?"

I busy myself making a tower out of the creamers.

She laughs. "I'm right, aren't I?"

"If this is your way to sweet-talk me into giving you the shot, you're going about it the wrong way."

She flicks my tower, and it crumbles. "Come on. Talk to me. Use me."

"Use you?"

"Get your mind out of the gutter. Is that all you think about now, sex?"

"I'm not the one trying to have a baby."

"Joke's on you because we're on a 'schedule.'" She puts schedule in air quotes. "Saving all that sperm for ovulation time."

I put my fingers in my ears and shake my head. She throws a creamer at me and it bounces off my forehead.

I sigh. "I do want a wife and kids. I'm not going to say I don't. But I don't want to marry the wrong woman, and if she had stuck around longer, maybe that could have happened with Leilani."

She leans in over the table. "You proposed to her?"

"No. Thank fuck I didn't."

"Yeah, that would've been a mistake. You'd be married to a felon right now and you could kiss that detective job bye-bye." She kisses her fingers and waves them.

"She's not a felon."

"She's about to be if she doesn't show up for her court date."

Luckily, I get a reprieve when our food arrives. She stares at her salad then back at my meal.

"No way," I say.

"Half? Half a salad would do you good."

I look at my stomach, thinking about the whole Jolie/Santa thing. "No."

"Knox, I love you. How about I promise to not give you grief tomorrow night at the retirement party? I won't even bug the waitress."

"I'll split it with you if you stop calling her the waitress."

She purses her lips and thinks about it for a moment. How could she not just agree? I pick up the burger take a big bite of it.

Her eyes narrow. "Fine."

"Say her name," I say.

"Kamea." She holds out her plate for me to put half the burger on it.

"Good girl." I cut the burger in half and place it on the plate, and she steals half the fries.

"Fries weren't part of the deal," I say.

She chomps down on one, not caring.

After we finish our meals, she wipes her mouth and pushes away her plate as though she ate a seven-course meal. "I was scared for a minute there."

"About what?"

"I thought for sure you'd try to duck out of the shots as a trade for the burger."

We pay the bill and get up from the table. "I'm still not giving you a shot."

She walks out before me. "We'll see about that."

I blow out a breath and shake my head. I wouldn't trade her for the world.

"Now let's talk about Kamea coming with you tomorrow night."

I turn the key in the ignition. "Let's not."

I don't tell her, but I've already thought about it enough for both of us. Mostly what kind of dress she borrowed from Sierra and how I'll hide my hard-on when I pick her up from Dylan and Rian's tomorrow evening.

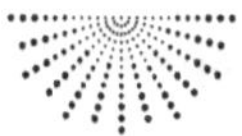

CHAPTER SEVENTEEN

Kamea

This feels like a lot more makeup than I usually wear. Rian's eyes widen when she looks at me.

"Let's remember Kamea has a natural glow about her," Rian says, and I give her my best thankful look.

"Yes. We're just enhancing it," Blanca says.

I can't argue, since I haven't seen my face. Blanca's makeup is usually flawless and fits her perfectly. I've never been much of a makeup person though, other than eyeliner and mascara. But it is a special occasion.

"Not to mention, Knox will be showing her off," Sierra adds, looking up from her magazine.

My gut twists. Show me off? I'm not the type of woman you show off. Hopefully I can get the cricket out of my throat long enough to actually speak to people.

"Make fish lips," Blanca says, and Evan refills my wine glass.

"Oh no, I can't have any more. As it is, I have to walk in those heels." I eye the shoes Sierra brought over. I could do a lot of harm with those spiky heels—mostly to myself.

"You look nervous. This will help." Blanca hands me the wine. "Before I put on the lipstick."

"I love makeovers," Sierra says, flipping through the magazine again.

Dylan walks into the apartment. His gaze falls over the wine, the makeup all over his kitchen table, and someone on each piece of furniture. He grunts and disappears into his bedroom.

"Yeah, I'll be…" Rian stands.

"Dealing with crabby man? Yeah, we got ya." Sierra shuts the magazine. "Kamea, do you think that maybe you and Knox might…"

"What?" Evan asks.

"Sleep together," Sierra says as if it's nothing.

I'm not made for this. Why did I agree to this? I have to meet all these people and lie about dating Knox. I wouldn't mind dating Knox, but he had his chance and chose not to go for it. I don't hold a grudge about it. When he apologized, I accepted it because what else can I do?

I just wish he wasn't so flirtatious lately. Our looks tend to linger a little longer since our conversation on the rooftop. He doesn't shy away when he's in my way anymore but allows me to slide by him, our bodies touching. I feel as if someone has nestled the kindling together for a fire and they're hovering over it with the knife and flint.

"No, this is fake," I say.

Sierra rolls her eyes. "So what? All this shit Leilani put you through, you deserve a night of fun that includes being limp in his bed tomorrow morning."

Evan laughs, and Blanca gives me a smile to say that Sierra is just being Sierra.

"Lip time, so she can't talk anymore." Blanca winks and puts on my lipstick. Once she's done, she steps back, appraising her work. "You look beautiful."

"Thanks," I say.

"Don't thank me until you see it." She holds out her hand for me to go to the bathroom.

Rian emerges from the bedroom as I walk past her to the bathroom. I look in the mirror and I can hardly believe it's me. Although I felt as though Blanca was layering my makeup like a five-tier cake, it's not overpowering. It kind of makes me feel sexy and beautiful.

A knock lands on the apartment door, and Blanca jogs over. "Don't come out until we tell you."

I nod.

I hear the door open and Rian says, "Hello, are you here to pick up Kamea?"

The other girls laugh, and Knox says, "Cut the act. What did you do with her?"

I step out, not about making my reveal a big deal. This is a fake date. The girls want it to be more than it is. But his head turns and his gaze takes me in. Without saying a word, he steps toward me, the two of us soaking the other in. He's wearing a dark suit—I can't tell if it's dark gray or black—a white shirt, and a pinstripe tie. It's the flush on his cheeks I can't stop staring at. Is he as nervous as me?

"You look great. You ready?" He holds out his hand.

I slide my hand into his large one. "Yeah."

"Bye, everyone." He waves to the girls.

"Thank you for everything," I say.

"The dress looks *gorgeous* on you," Sierra says, her eyes on the back of Knox's head. "Keep it because I'll never be able to wear it without thinking of how *stunning* you are in it."

"Don't go breaking my buddy's heart now," Dylan says from the bedroom doorway, his arms crossed.

"Can't break a heart that isn't invested," I joke.

Knox stops for a moment before opening the front door for me.

"Bye, you guys. Don't worry, we won't wait up," Evan says, giggling.

The door shuts, and Knox and I walk to the elevator without saying a word.

Once we're in the elevator car, Knox's gaze falls down my body again. "I got us an Uber because I wasn't going to put you in the Bronco looking like that."

"Okay."

The elevator descends and the doors slide open. He waits for me to get out and points toward the Uber we're taking to the party. I slide in first and he slides in beside me. Knox makes small talk with the driver while his hand stays dangerously close to mine. I rack my brain for anything I've done to make him act like this. He's doing everything right, but he feels colder, more distant than normal.

When we get out, I put my hand on his arm. "Am I missing something?"

"Like what?"

"You haven't really talked to me."

His shoulders fall and I prepare myself for the worst. What is he about to say?

"Sorry. I think I'm just nervous." He wipes his hands down the front of his slacks.

"About how I'll do? I'll do my best to make a good impression, you have my word."

"God, no." His hand touches my shoulder. "This party is big for me. I have to make a great impression, otherwise the detective job is smoke. But it's not you I'm worried about."

Thank God, because I was about a second away from climbing back in that Uber and having him keep on driving.

"Thanks for coming," Knox says. "You look gorgeous. I'm afraid you're going to be distracting."

"Isn't that a good thing?" I walk in front of him.

He catches up, placing his hand on the small of my back. "Not when I have to zero my attention in on my boss."

"Remind me, how convincing do you want me to be?" I ask, unsure if I should act like his cousin. "I mean hand-holding, kisses on the cheek, too much?"

He smiles at me. "Play it however you're comfortable and I'll make sure I match you."

"Perfect."

He opens the glass door and I file in first, but when his body slides in close and his strong chest is a form of support, I sigh. Tonight might be fun, but I'm sure I'll suffer the consequences tomorrow.

<hr>

WE'RE WAITING for dinner to be served when I slide my hand under the table and rest it on Knox's knee. His arm is over the back of my chair, his fingers fiddling with a strand of my hair that Blanca curled.

"Did Knox tell you he has to give me shots?" Patrice says, and her husband gives her a death stare.

I glance at Knox as he shakes his head. "I told you I'm not doing it."

She waves him off. "We're trying to have a baby," she whispers and eyes the other side of the table.

The two guys seated with us keep looking at me and then their phones. Their wives are talking nonstop about kids and school.

"That's great," I say.

"But Knox needs to give me a fertility shot during our shift." Patrice clenches her teeth.

Knox's body doesn't show any discomfort with Patrice's displeasure.

"I'm sure he'll do it."

"Nope," Knox says as though he's half in the conversation and half out of the conversation. I squeeze his leg, and he slides his thigh closer to me and tugs on my strand of hair. "I said no."

"Are you her sister?" one of the guys says from across the table.

Here we go again.

"No, she's not," Knox answers for me. "DuPont, put the damn phone away."

Surprisingly, they do, but I think it has more to do with the meals being placed in front of us than Knox's request. I sit up straighter, seeing chicken and steak on my plate. I glance at Knox.

He cringes. "Sorry."

"It's okay," I say.

"It is?" he asks.

"Yeah, could you just take them off my plate? I'll eat the mashed potatoes and vegetables."

He takes the meat off my plate, but then he flags down a waiter. "Do you guys have a vegetarian option? I must've ordered wrong for my date."

The man looks at me and takes my plate away. "I'll be right back."

Knox sits there while everyone else eats.

"Eat," I whisper to him.

"No, I'll wait."

"Yours will get cold."

"It's fine. It won't take much time to eat it." He sips his beer.

Patrice talks about how her husband would've prepared

such a better meal. Five minutes later, the two men across the table are already done.

I pinch Knox's thigh. "Eat."

"No." He exaggerates the no.

Just when I'm about to pick up his fork and cut his meat for him like a child, the server returns with a plate pretty much full of vegetables, but I'll take it.

"We'll stop somewhere on the way home," Knox whispers in my ear. I appreciate his offer, but his breath in my eardrum is increasing my libido.

I use my fork and knife to cut up my green beans as though they're a steak. I'm used to not being catered to at a big event like this, and I'm happy to eat whatever they offer. The group at our table talks about the detective retiring, and the guy across the table who thinks I look like Leilani tells Knox that he's up against some tough competition for the detective's position.

"He's got it," Patrice says. "No better cop out there than Whelan." She winks at her partner.

Knox reaches behind me to fist-bump her.

"No other applicant with an ex-girlfriend they just had to arrest." Both guys laugh.

Knox stiffens but surprisingly says nothing. Maybe I'm typecasting, but Knox is so big and muscular that I expected he'd slide out his chair and ask the guy to go outside. But he cuts his steak and remains silent.

"She got arrested for protecting animal rights," I say.

"Don't entertain them," Knox whispers to me.

"Shooting a man in the nuts isn't protecting animal rights," the guy with the receding hairline says.

I shrug. "So she has bad aim."

"Good catch, Whelan. Sounds like this one will be in the cell right next to the first one."

"Go to hell," Knox says.

"First of all." I place my silverware down. "I'm not suggesting what she did was smart. It was reckless, but passionate all the same. But whether it was right or wrong, it says nothing about Knox. He wasn't with her. Surely if you divorced your wife and she got mad at the traffic mom one school morning and punched her in the face, that wouldn't be a reflection on you. Would it?"

"Sweetie, I'd never do that," the one wife says.

"I'd run the bitch over," the other wife says and sips from her wine glass.

The men only look amused, not understanding my point. Maybe Knox was right and I'm just wasting my breath, but I refuse to sit here and blame Knox when none of it was under his control.

"Here comes the person you really have to convince anyway." The man smiles at someone behind us. "Cap."

A large hand falls on Knox's shoulders. "Whelan, you want to introduce me to your date?"

Knox wipes his mouth and sets his napkin on the table, sliding out his chair. "Captain, this is Kamea. Kamea, this is Captain Donnelly."

Now the real work begins.

CHAPTER EIGHTEEN

Knox

Captain Donnelly laughs at Kamea's joke about being a vegetarian and living with Jax and me.

"My third ex was a vegetarian and I will say I did enjoy this fried tofu thing she'd make."

I pass drinks to Cap and Kamea from the bar.

"When I first started eating tofu, I didn't know there are so many different consistencies and one time I wanted to pan fry the soft kind and well, the fire alarm for the entire building ended up going off." He chuckles again. "My second wife was the worst cook. I finally took out the batteries from the fire alarms because they'd go off when she was making a pizza." He leans in close to Kamea. "Don't tell that to the fire department though."

Kamea zips her lips and pretends she's throwing the key away.

This entire time, I thought she was shy. That I'd bring her

here tonight and she'd barely talk to a soul. But she was ready to go rounds with Milliken and now she's winning over Cap.

How can anyone resist her?

She's drop-dead gorgeous tonight. She is every day, but I almost couldn't talk when I walked into Rian's earlier. I had to remind myself that she isn't mine, that this is all pretend.

Then again, after the rooftop talk, I can't help but think about what would happen if we crossed that line. I have to remind myself I'd never do that to her because she's staying with us.

A clap on my back interrupts my thoughts and I blink to find Cap and Kamea staring at me.

"Go out on the balcony," Cap says. "They have heaters, and someone said the snow was floating down. I need to go find the wife before she ends up drunk on champagne. She loves the bubbly." He shakes Kamea's hand. "It was quite the pleasure."

"You as well."

"And I'll definitely be in touch for the T-shirts for our district basketball team." He twirls her card in his hand.

How long was I not paying attention?

"Sounds great. I'll be at the first game to see you dunk."

Captain laughs and points his finger as if Kamea is a comedian. He leaves us, giving me a thumbs-up behind Kamea's back. Some of the tension leaves my body. I definitely made the right decision bringing her tonight.

"Want to go outside?" I ask.

She glances at the balcony where a few people are gathered. "Sure, although I wish I had your hot cider." She hooks her arm through mine, and I lead her to the doors.

The cool rush of air when we get outside almost has me turning us around, but I shrug off my jacket and place it over her shoulders. "Better?"

She touches my jacket and looks at me with so much appreciation, my heart jerks. Sometimes Kamea is everything I want in a woman, but I have no idea how to approach the subject with her or if I even should.

"Thank you," she says.

We stand by a heater on the balcony that looks over the riverfront of Cliffton Heights.

"I think I like Cliffton Heights more than Peekskil," she says.

"How did you end up in Peekskil, by the way?"

She sighs and her eyes focus on the riverfront illuminated by lights along the sidewalk. During summer months, people hang out there, but not tonight. "Well, I came to New York after college graduation and had a few jobs in New York City, but then I yearned for something smaller. So I came out to the suburbs and got that job where we first met. Then a friend of a friend and I ended up in Peekskil somehow. Sometimes I feel like I'm barely hanging on in life, you know? Like, when is my time going to come?"

I move in closer to her and sip my beer. "Yeah, I feel the same when it comes to the cop thing. Because of where I came from, I surprised the shit out of my old friends that someone like me would be a cop. I'd be fine being a street cop for the rest of my life, but I want to be a detective. I think I could do a good job."

"At least you have a career."

"You have the T-shirt thing."

She gives me a look and rolls her eyes. "Exactly. A T-shirt thing. Not a company."

I knock my shoulder to her arm. "Don't do that to yourself. You're talented and you're going to make something of it. One day I'll be telling people, I knew her once. Saved her from sleeping under an overpass one night."

She laughs It rings through the cold air and my heart warms at the sound.

"That's why I did it," she jokes. "So that one day when I'm famous, I can say I worked my way up, you know? I had no money and was sleeping on the streets. Keeping out the fact that it was only one night. Because a cop saved me and gave me a roof to sleep under. It's a good backstory, no?"

I laugh. She's talented, and I hate that she doesn't believe in herself.

"Why did you?" she asks. "Take me in."

"I told you, it's not safe for you to be on the streets."

She turns toward me, leaning her side against the metal railing. "Is it because I bailed Leilani out? Like you feel somehow responsible?"

I blink in surprise. I wish for one night we could keep Leilani out of our conversations. If only Kamea never knew her, we could pretend we were strangers with no common link.

"No." I shake my head. "I just did it because you're a young, beautiful woman." I wink.

"So you would've saved anyone?"

"Yeah. For sure." I shrug.

"But Dell is on the street…"

She brings up a woman who could probably take me down if she really wanted to. Dell scares me, but I'm not admitting that to anyone.

Instead, I say, "Dell wants to be on the street."

"Oh. So if I had fought harder, you would've left me?" The way her lips are tipped up, I think she's playing me.

"No." I step closer, my hand finding her hip.

"Why then?" she whispers.

"Because it was you."

"Me?"

My fingers tighten on her hip and I nudge her closer so

there's barely any space between us. "Yeah. All those years ago, I'm gonna be honest here, I made the wrong choice that night. It should've been you. And I'd do just about anything to have a do-over."

A barely audible sound falls from her lips. "What?" There's a hint of disbelief in her question.

"I should've taken you home that night. You're the one who fits me."

"Knox." She steps back and turns around, away from my hold. "What are you saying?"

I step up behind her. "I want you. I want you in every way possible, but I won't cross the line, Kamea. Not now."

"Why not?" She slowly turns to face me again. "Why did you just tell me all that then?"

I have no idea why I laid my heart out there. Maybe I wanted it off my chest and she's the one I trust the most. Maybe because I want her to know that I regret that decision. That Leilani didn't bring me anything but heartache. Seeing Kamea tonight and the entire time she's been living with us, she fits perfectly in my life.

"Because I wanted you to know," I say.

She steps closer, her breasts pressing to my chest. "And why aren't you going to act on it?"

"Because you're staying with us and I can't jeopardize that. I don't want you thinking you have to be with me to have a roof over your head. Nor do I want you to think you have to feel the same way as me."

"And if I do?" Her fingers run down my tie. "If I feel the same way? If I think you were an idiot all those years ago, but I want to start over, like that never happened?"

"I'd say we'll put it on the back burner until we find her and get your money back. When you're back on your feet."

She shakes her head. "You're used to dictating everything, aren't you? Is that because you're a cop?"

She has a point. I tend to dictate how I want things to go. I like it that way. "Yes."

"Well, Officer Whelan, you're not going to control this situation. Because I'm a grown woman and although I love your intentions, it's my decision."

"Kamea," I plead, but she grabs my tie and pulls me down.

"Kiss me, Knox," she whispers, her lips millimeters from mine.

"Kamea," I plea again, but the pull between us is so strong, I can't resist when she presses her lips to mine.

Damn, they're soft and tender. She holds her lips against mine, knowing I can't wait long before I lick along the seam of her lips, and she opens for me. My tongue tangles with hers. She tastes and feels amazing. She's not tentative or shy, and her moan has me about falling to my knees to worship her, if only for more sounds like that. My fingers dig into her hips and my erection presses against her stomach.

"This one is going to be arrested for public indecency," a deep voice says from behind us.

I push Kamea away from me and allow my breath to even out.

"Leave the lovebirds alone, sweetie," a woman says.

I'm not even going to turn around to see who it is. My mind swims with leftover sensations from that kiss and how amazing it was. It ignited a spark I'm not sure will ever go out.

"Is that convincing enough for you?" she asks.

I shake my head. "We can't. We shouldn't have."

Her face falls and she takes off my coat and hands it back to me. "You regret it?"

I pull on the back of my neck. "It's not right."

"Because I'm living with you?"

"Yes, don't you see that?"

She shouldn't want to start whatever this is between us

when she'd be the one on the street if it goes bad. Not that I'd allow that, but the apartment is mine, not hers. She needs to be more protective of herself.

"Okay. Fine." She walks away.

"Where are you going?" I ask.

"To see about cake. It's the next best thing to an orgasm."

She disappears inside, and my head falls back, wondering how I manage to keep screwing things up with this woman. I follow her inside, but when I find Kamea, she's got a slice of cake on a plate and she's talking to Patrice. From the evil stare coming from Patrice, I'm guessing I'm not welcome to join that conversation.

For the rest of the night, Kamea is polite enough, but once we're in an Uber, the silent treatment commences.

At our apartment door, I say, "Thanks for going with me."

"Sure thing." She walks in and is about to go into her room, but she turns back around, lifting her long hair off her neck. "Could you do one last thing and unzip me?"

"Yeah, sure."

My fingers go to her zipper and I lower it. It goes down to her mid ass, which means I'm looking at her in a thong. A black thong that reveals her amazing ass. Fucking hell. Why can't I be a douchebag? If there was ever a time for me to be one, now is it.

She steps away before my fingers even leave the zipper. "Thanks. Good night, Knox."

She walks into her bedroom and shuts the door.

You could be in there naked with her, dumbass.

"Night," I whisper.

CHAPTER NINETEEN

Kamea

*L*ucky for me, I'm the first one awake on Saturday morning. Instead of working on my T-shirts—which is what I should do—I decide to play a little game with Knox.

I get in my yoga pants and sweatshirt, put on a cap, and take the elevator down to street level. I cross the street and walk right into Sweet Infusion. It's hectic and Rian is breezing from the front to the back. Customers are waiting by the pick-up station.

"Do you need help?" I ask her since there's no one else here.

"Oh my God, yes! Pour some coffee, or if you want to go in the back and grab the muffins I just made, that would be great."

"I'm good with the coffee pouring," I say and grab a pot. Then I notice a list of tickets for specialty drinks. I pick up a ticket and hold it up for her. "What about these?"

"Yeah, I'll be back to make those. Dylan's in the shower and then he's coming over."

"I'll make them."

"You know how?" she asks.

"Country club folks love their fancy coffee drinks."

She laughs. "I owe you whatever you want." She disappears into the kitchen.

Well, I hope she remembers that promise when I tell her my plan.

I prepare the coffees and get orders out to a few people who thank me. Rian comes out with a tray of muffins right when Dylan walks in, freshly showered.

"What do you need, babe?" he asks Rian.

"I had another savior." She smiles at me before kissing Dylan quickly.

Dylan nods at me. "Hey, Kamea."

"Hi, Dylan." I lift my arm in a wave. Lately, I've been getting some bad vibes from Dylan and I'm not entirely sure why. I've barely ever talked to the guy.

"Thanks, Kamea. Dylan can take over."

A customer comes over to the pick-up ledge and holds up his latte. "This is the best one I've ever had." He smiles at me.

I nod. "Thank you."

"I'll be back tomorrow." He leaves.

Rian gapes at me. "Um… that man complains about everything every time he comes in. What did you do?"

I shrug. "I just made him a latte."

"Show me," she says and leaves Dylan.

"I'll manage the register. Is there anything in the back you need me to do?" Dylan puts on an apron that says, "I belong to the baker."

"Nope. Everything we have is out now."

I show Rian how I make my lattes, though I don't really think it's that different from anyone else. Twenty minutes later, another rush comes in. I'll give it to Dylan—he manages the front end without hardly needing Rian, allowing us to work on all the drinks.

After it slows down, Dylan grabs a croissant and sits down with a coffee and his phone.

"Did all your help call in?" I ask Rian.

She nods. "Yeah, that's high schoolers for you, right? During the week, I have a few moms who come in the morning and get all the big orders together with me. I'm really going to have to rethink who I'm hiring."

"Well, you can keep me on standby. I don't have any hours at the country club, what with them closing for renovations until the spring. Besides that, I only have my T-shirts."

"Oh!" She touches my arm. "I was talking to Jax and he said you did some specialty T-shirts for him?"

I nod because he swore me to secrecy, but once he actually has them, I plan on disappearing. Frankie might just kick my ass.

"Could you do some for the shop?"

I nod. "What are you thinking?"

"I'll come by tonight and we can talk about it?"

I glance at Dylan, who isn't paying us any attention. "I had a favor to ask you actually."

Her shoulders fall. "What?"

"It's kind of a long story." I glance at Dylan again. "Could we talk in the kitchen?"

"Sure." She walks toward the kitchen, and I follow her.

Once we're in there, I feel more comfortable telling her everything that went down with Knox and me on the balcony last night. The things he said, the declaration that he should've picked me. That it's something he regrets. And that kiss. My body is still pulsing from that kiss. His lips were so firm and demanding, but at the same time, he wasn't pressuring me. The way his hands held my hips and the feel of his erection. God help me.

By the time I finish, Rian's hand is over her heart. "Oh, Knox."

I nod. "I figure if I move in with you guys just to prove my point, we'll see if he makes a move."

"And what if he doesn't?" She's right to worry about that. Knox is a hard man to predict.

"Then he never really wanted me anyway."

"It's a game with a lot of moving pieces."

I nod. "Would Dylan be okay with it?"

"Oh, please." She waves. "These guys do so much shit to get their friends to get out of their own stubborn ways. Jax acted like he liked me for a while just to get Dylan jealous enough to make a move on me."

"So when he leaves for work tonight, we'll move my stuff over?" I ask.

She nods. "And I'll fill Dylan in."

"Great. Thanks so much, Rian."

I give her a quick hug, and she forces a box of muffins on me before I walk out of the kitchen.

"Hey, Kamea," she says.

I turn around to face her.

"I'm impressed. You always seemed like this shy girl who lets things happen to her and didn't make them happen for herself. Go, girl!"

I laugh. "Thanks."

Let's just hope this turns out how I want.

I'M at the breakfast counter, working on a new T-shirt line devoted to women who want to be in charge of their own destinies. It's different from what I usually do, but I'm feeling inspired.

Knox comes out of his room, dressed in sweatpants and a T-shirt. "Did Rian deliver these?" He opens the bakery box and takes a bran muffin. Even a muffin has to be semi-healthy for this guy.

"No, I was over there this morning and she gave them to me to bring back."

He sits down and glances at my computer. "What's that?"

I turn my computer more toward me. "Just something I'm working on."

He sighs. "I don't want this to be weird. The whole reason we didn't do anything was so it wouldn't be weird."

I shut my computer and get up, going to the fridge. I grab the orange juice. "That's funny, because if you *had* crossed the line, we'd probably be naked in one of those rooms right now. But you have rules, and everyone needs to follow them, right?"

His mouth opens, but he says nothing. Am I being a tad ridiculous? Yes. I can admit that. But his reasons for not doing anything about his attraction to me are stupid. I'm a grown woman and I understand the chance I'm taking if I sleep with him.

I'll be honest and say it wouldn't be my smartest decision, since I don't have anywhere else to go should things go bad. But that's not what he's worried about. He's worried that I somehow associate living here with having to sleep with him. What planet does he live on?

He sets down his muffin. "You're playing dirty."

"Dirty would be if I stripped down and walked around naked."

He swallows hard and his gaze zeroes in on my lips. "I'm not sure I know what you want me to do."

I shrug. "Nothing. I'm fine. Everything is fine."

"Fine. The woman's definition isn't the same as a man's."

I smile and turn because he's so right. "I just meant I understand your rules, but I don't have to like them or even agree with them."

Jax comes out of his room in just his boxers. "What's up, guys? How was last night?"

"Fine," I say.

Jax looks at Knox with a cringe.

"See, even Jax knows what it means when a woman says it's fine." Knox motions to Jax.

"Let's get his take on it then, huh?" I finish off my orange juice.

"Where did that sweet girl who lived with us go?" Jax asks.

I ignore his questions. "So, Jax, let's say you like a girl. And you help her out with a place to stay. Things are going well. You flirt with her. She flirts with you. You look at her every morning like you want to rip her clothes off, and she looks at you like you're her personal lollipop she wants to suck on when you come out of the shower."

"Just so I'm clear, this is you two we're talking about, right?" He points two fingers between us.

"No," Knox says at the same time as I say, "Yes."

"Okay, carry on." Jax sits down where I was sitting.

"You go on a fake date, but during the course of the night, you admit you have feelings for her. And you kiss her. And it's a really amazing kiss. But then you say you can't do anything more because she's a loser who doesn't have a place to live and you gave her a place to live and if you guys act on those feelings, then she'll think she has to be with you to continue to stay at your place."

Jax laughs and clasps Knox on the shoulder. "Welcome to Whelanville. Full of morals and rules. He knows best and don't try to change his mind."

"That's unfair. Tell her this is legit. A good reason for this." Knox stands.

"We're cut from a different cloth, man, you know this. I would've fucked her the first night she was here." Jax lifts his wrist to look at an imaginary watch. "We're, what? Day I have no idea, but you should've fucked her already."

"He should have last night," I say.

Knox stares at me for a second. "I agree with Jax. Who are you and what have you done with our sweet Kamea?"

"I think she's buried under the animosity of you denying her an orgasm last night." Jax holds up both hands and backs up. "At least that's what it seems to me." He goes to the bathroom, and we hear him peeing a second later.

"Jesus Christ, shut the fucking door." Knox walks over to the bathroom, grabs the handle, and slams the door.

I grab my computer and head to my room. "Have a great shift today, Knox."

He says nothing, but his eyes convey he doesn't understand what's going on.

Once I'm behind my bedroom door, I regret being so forceful, but I hate when people think they know what's best for me. The fact he's holding me behind velvet ropes pisses me off. I won't admit this to him, but I'm pissed at myself too. I put myself in a position where some guy thinks he can't be with me because I'm too vulnerable. It's about time I do what I'm designing on these new shirts—I need to be a girl boss.

I lift the screen on my laptop. Time to make some money and get the hell out of here. Regardless of where things go with Knox.

CHAPTER TWENTY

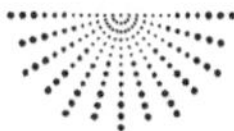

Knox

It's seven thirty in the morning when I step off the elevator of my apartment building. I had a shitty shift since Patrice called in sick—something about the fertility medicine not agreeing with her. It's another reminder that once she's pregnant, I won't have her as my partner and how much I really want that detective position. Interviews start next week.

When I enter my apartment, something feels off, but I can't put my finger on it.

I make myself some eggs, mentally telling myself we're low on groceries. Neither Jax nor Kamea come out, which is odd. Usually Kamea is up and working on her computer when I get home. But maybe it's for the best, since she's pissed at me. Hopefully she'll calm down after a few days. I know I'm right about what I said.

After cleaning the kitchen, I go into the bathroom and

take a shower. It looks so bare in here. Maybe Kamea ran out of her shampoo and conditioner because her bottles are gone.

I dry off afterward and notice that her robe is no longer on the back hook of the door. Walking out of the bathroom, I spot Jax rounding the kitchen area with his mug of coffee.

"Morning," he says and presses the button on the TV remote.

I thumb toward the bathroom door. "Hey, the bathroom seems pretty empty."

"Yeah. Kamea moved out." He sips his coffee, his attention on the television.

My stomach drops. "What?"

"Across the hall to Rian and Dylan's." He turns his head to look at me. "It's your fault. You and your rules."

"My rules? Whatever, man. Think about it, you know I'm right."

He sets down his coffee, clasps his hands, and stares at me. "You're being an idiot. You ruined your chance with her once already and now you're blowing it again. Don't you like her?"

I sit on the couch and lean back, running my hands through my hair. I do. I know I do. I should've never asked her to move in with us. Because I already felt that wave of arousal running through me when she was near. And now I'm the one pushing her away. I nod.

"Then stop being a pussy."

"But what if it's… what if…"

Jax sighs. "She's not Leilani. At all. She's sweet and kind and takes you as you are. Hell, she moved out just to prove this stupid point to you."

"Why would she do that?"

"My first inclination is to say because we're back in sixth grade. But I think she did it because she likes you."

"She likes me," I murmur.

"Yes, and right now, you're making her look like an idiot. If you keep doing that, you can kiss any chance with her goodbye forever." He turns to face me. "I get that Leilani hurt you. And you might not agree, but the girl wasn't worth it. Do you still have feelings for her?"

"No. This has nothing to do with Leilani," I say, and I know that's the truth. All I think about is Kamea all the time.

"Then go get the girl you want. We both know if things with you guys don't work out, you're not going to kick her out. So don't use that excuse anymore." He stands and lifts his coffee mug, going to his room. "I have to go get ready to leave because Jolie swindled me into helping her Daisy Scout troop with some scavenger hunt thing."

"You're helping out?" I ask with a note of disbelief.

"Because jackass can't be a real father. She asked and I'm not going to turn down the girl. I remember how much all those damn father-son and mother-son days sucked for me."

I nod, getting now why he would help. "Have fun."

He huffs. "Fun with a bunch of kindergarteners? I'm not sure there's such a thing."

He shuts his bedroom door and I realize Jax is right. It's time I take what I want without thinking of the repercussions. When I was with Leilani, I second-guessed every decision I made—mostly because I was worried that I'd scare her off. But Kamea is different and we're different together. It's time I give in to the pull I feel toward her and own it like I should've before Leilani ever came into my life.

I HEAD into my bedroom and get dressed in my jeans and shirt. Then I knock on Rian and Dylan's door.

He opens it right away. "Finally. What took you so long?" He steps aside. "Catch her before she's unpacked."

I narrow my eyes at Dylan. What the hell is his problem?

Rian walks out of what used to be Dylan's room and before that Sierra's. She holds up her hand. "Sorry, you're not welcome."

"What?" My forehead scrunches.

"You heard me."

"It's fine, Rian," Kamea says from inside the room.

Rian steps aside with a glare that's not at all like her.

I step into Dylan's old room and shut the door. The bed is made. Kamea's television sits on the dresser. Every time one of our friends moves out because they've found the love of their life, they leave behind furniture. This is all Sierra's shit, so the room suits Kamea a lot more than Seth's ratty chair.

"Why did you move out?" I ask, sitting on the bed while she walks back and forth between the closet and the bed, hanging up clothes. Every single one of her items is in here.

"Well, you made it clear we couldn't do anything with both of us under the same roof. So I made a deal with Rian."

"Deal?"

She nods. "I'm her new coffee person every morning in exchange for living here."

"Seriously?"

She smiles at me, all sweet and condescending. "Well, I think she would've allowed me to move in even if I didn't take the job, but I couldn't do that."

I scratch my head. "Okay. Um… I appreciate the effort, but why don't you just come back? Maybe I was rash in my decision-making."

"Rash?" she asks, turning around with a shirt on a hanger in her hand. "I'd hate for you to break one of your self-imposed rules."

"Cut the shit, Kamea." I'm losing patience. Although I can admit that this whole thing is turning me on a bit.

"What? I'm just trying to figure out a way that we could give this a shot." The voice she's using is too innocent.

My jaw clenches. "Come over here and sit." I pat the bed next to me.

"I have a lot to do. I hate being unsettled." She grabs another shirt and hangs it up. Her closet isn't as full as a normal girl's, which I fucking hate. She deserves everything, including a closet full of clothes and too many shoes.

"Kamea," I say.

"Knox," she mimics me.

I blow out a breath. "Sit, please."

"Please?"

"Yes, please." I pat the spot next to me.

She hangs up the sweater and sits on the edge of the bed. "What's up?"

"You know exactly what's up."

"I do?" Her smile says she's unable to keep up the act when we're face to face.

"You don't have to move out. Let's get all your stuff and go back to our place."

"Your place," she says. "And I like it here. Rian is super sweet, and this way, you don't have to worry that I'm only screwing you in exchange for a roof over my head."

I groan and she laughs, standing. I grab her wrist and yank her to me. She falls between my legs and my hands mold to her hips.

"Are you sure about this?" I ask, my heart racing with the thought of putting myself out there again.

"About what?" The fact that her lips are tipped into a devilish grin says she knows exactly what I'm saying, but she wants me to spell it out.

"Us. Giving this a shot. Discovering what this is between us."

Her fingers run through the hair at the side of my head and my eyes close briefly from the contact.

"What's between us?" she asks in a low voice.

I pick her up and throw her onto the bed, covering my body with hers. With her hands locked above her head, I lower my lips toward hers but stop right before I allow them to meet. She licks her lips.

"The fact I want to kiss you, bite you, touch you, fuck you. You're all I can think of and I'm sorry about the rules, but I'm a cop, okay? I live by rules."

She nods. Kamea wiggles her arms until I release her, then she wraps them around my neck. "So we'll give this an honest shot?"

"Yeah."

"Then show me."

"Show you what?" I ask.

"Show me how much you want me. Unless—"

I crash my lips to hers, her body wiggling under mine while I slide on top of her. Her thighs part and my hips fall between them, my hands brushing her hair away as our tongues glide together. She raises one leg and I grind into her, rewarded with an earth-quaking moan slipping from her throat.

I tear my lips from her mouth, my thumb running down the center of her throat. My lips touch her jaw and neck before traveling down her body. She's wearing one of her T-shirts about her being powered by plants, and I slide my hand up the hem. Her body shivers under my touch, so I look up to make sure we're on the same page.

"You okay?" I ask.

Her cheeks hold a slight tinge of pink and her hooded eyes say she's into this, but I need verbal affirmation.

"Yeah, it's just been a while for me."

I slide down her body, my hands staying on her ribcage. "It's been a while for me too. I haven't really been dating or anything."

"But what about sex?" she asks with an arched brow.

I'm not exactly proud of my behavior after Leilani left me. I screwed around with a few random girls I probably wouldn't have otherwise, but it's been months since then. But in order for Kamea to know that this is different, I need to have this conversation with her.

I sit up. "You should know that after the breakup, I did sleep with a few women. All I wanted was her out of my head. But this thing between us isn't the same thing. I want to be with you now, tomorrow, and the next day. There's nothing quick about this. And if you want to wait, I'm cool. We can go out on a date, a real one."

She nods, but her mind is clearly whizzing.

"I want to pursue this with you, but that doesn't mean just physically."

"So you don't want to have sex with me?"

I laugh and run a hand through my hair. "Of course I do. But making this work long term is more important to me than getting you into bed this instant."

"Perfect answer, Officer Whelan." She straddles my lap. "Take me to your apartment. I don't want to piss off my new roommates because I have a feeling things are about to get a little loud."

"Your wish is my command." I pick her up and walk us out of the bedroom.

Dylan and Rian are at the kitchen table.

"Made up, I see?" Rian asks with a smirk.

"You forgot her boxes," Dylan says, and Rian smacks him.

"Later," I say and Kamea opens the door for us to go through.

Jax is about to lock up the apartment when he spots us. "Thank fuck, I'm headed out." He disappears down the hall.

I don't stop until we're in my bedroom, where I lower her to my bed. Her long dark hair is strewn over my pillow. Her pink cheeks and hot body call to me. If I went through all that hell to be here right now, with her, it was all worth it. She's worth it.

CHAPTER TWENTY-ONE

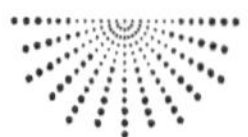

Kamea

Knox stares down at me as if I'm something he's craved for ages. His look alone spurs wetness between my legs. He's made it so easy for me to get lost in him. The stunt I pulled might have been juvenile, but it got us here, and from the lust in his eyes, he wants to be here.

"Knox," I say in a quivering voice.

It has been a long time for me, and it unnerved me, hearing that after Leilani, he slept around. But we all have our past and the only thing that matters is now.

He reaches back and tears off his shirt, leaving his chest bare for my inspecting eyes. No other man I've been with has looked like Knox. Never so built and muscular.

I sit up and slide to the end of the bed, and he steps forward. My hands fumble with his jeans, unbuttoning and unzipping them.

When I look up at him, he pushes his hand through my hair, his tongue sweeping along his bottom lip. "I want you so bad."

The way he says it has me pressing my thighs together. Hooking my fingers into the waistband of his jeans, I slide them over his ass, and they fall to the floor, leaving me eye level with his dick bulging in his boxer briefs.

"Seems unfair, right?"

I don't register what he's saying until he kicks off his pants and falls to his knees. He slowly raises my shirt up and over my head, leaving me in my ivory bralette that leaves nothing to the imagination. A groan erupts out of him. His hands mold to my breasts, his thumbs running over my peaked nipples. His fingers fall between my legs, sliding one along my center, the yoga pants barely a barrier.

"God, I want you." He stands up halfway and crashes his lips to mine. "I want to be inside of you," he says between kisses, rubbing me harder over the thin fabric. "I have to see you, taste you, devour you."

My back falls to the mattress and his hands slide to the waistband of my yoga pants. As though he can't take it anymore, he sits up on his knees and yanks them and my panties down in one shot, tossing them to the floor.

"Open for me." His hands glide up my quaking thighs, opening me for his examination. He growls, and my body responds with an ache of longing between my thighs.

"Please," I say, not above begging at this point.

But he grabs my ankles and tugs me to the edge of the bed. When I realize what he has planned, I shake my head. I've never been terribly comfortable with a guy going down on me. It's always felt like more of an obligation than a privilege on their part.

"No. I need you. I want to feel you," I say.

"You're crazy if you think I'm not going to taste you first.

I've been thinking about this since the moment you stepped back into my life."

My head falls down on the mattress when his fingers run down my slit and he pushes them inside me.

"That's what I thought," he says in a jovial tone.

When he latches his mouth to my clit, a wave of wonderment runs through my body. Holy shit, that feels good. He says nothing, and I don't have the nerve to look at him while he's doing it.

He swings my legs over his shoulders and his big arms wrap around my waist, pulling me flush to him. His tongue slowly adds more pressure. I grind, needing friction on my clit, needing him to take me where no man ever has in this position.

He groans and his fingers tighten on my hips. It's almost game over, and he must sense it because he concentrates on my clit, flicking it with his tongue and sucking on it. One hand disappears off my hip and he delves inside me, in and out until my body is flailing like a fish. But instead of begging for air, I'm begging for an orgasm.

Then I can't clench hard enough to delay it. As my climax hits, my head pushes into the mattress and I give in, allowing my orgasm to take over my body. It's the best feeling I've had in ages. All the stress, all the worries dissipate from my body.

Knox doesn't leave between my legs though. Instead he licks me until I stop vibrating from the wake. Then he lifts himself off, strips off his boxer briefs, goes to the nightstand, and returns with a condom in hand.

I take the condom from his hands, ripping it open. "You've been working so hard, allow me." I roll the condom down his large length.

His hand cradles my cheek, his thumb running along my skin. "When you come... you're gorgeous."

My breath catches in my throat. Knox's lips meet mine as

he crawls on the bed, and I scoot up until he's on top of me, his knee nudging my thighs open. The tip of his dick is right there at my opening. This is it. I'm going to have sex with him, and after this, there'll be no turning back.

As though he can hear my inner thoughts, he looks up and brushes a hair from my forehead. "You okay?"

I nod and grab the back of his head. His lips fall to mine and I thrust my tongue into his mouth. He enters me slowly, never stopping our kiss. I inhale sharply when he's fully inside me. Nothing has felt so wondrous. I've never felt so full. He tears his lips off me and locks his gaze with mine as he draws out of me and pushes back in. My fingers clutch his shoulder blades from the force, and when he does it again, I clench and tighten my thighs around his waist.

He quickens the pace. I tilt my head up to allow him access to kiss me as he drives in and out of me with abandon. Our hands are everywhere, trying to quench the need that's been between us for weeks. Being in the moment with him, feeling what he's feeling, the noises he makes, the words he murmurs, it all sucks us into a tornado of sexual desire we're greedy to ride out.

My orgasm is coming on fast—maybe because I just came from his mouth. As though reading my thoughts, he rolls us and brings me on top of him, his hands molding to my hips. His eyes stare up at me gets me to the brink. I rock in the direction his hands on my hips take me, and in seconds, I'm barreling toward my climax, crying out.

He keeps up the pace while I clench around him, then his abs contract under my touch. He clenches so hard, he sits up and takes me in his arms, groaning then stilling inside me.

His hands run up my bare back and shivers chase his touch. "You're amazing. So beautiful. I want to see you come all the damn time."

I'm a sweaty mess as he kisses my neck and tells me how

hard he came. We unhook from one another, and he goes to the bathroom to discard the condom before returning.

He slides into bed and opens the sheet for me to follow him. "Take a nap with me?"

Although I have a million things I have to do, I can't deny him.

"And then after, we'll move your stuff back here," he mumbles, his eyes already drifting closed.

"I'm not moving back," I whisper.

"What?" His eyes fly open, and I laugh and shake my head. "Why not?"

"Because it's better this way."

He looks at me long and hard, clearly not happy, then pats my shoulder. "We'll talk after we sleep. Just a few hours."

His hand nestles along my body, sliding me closer. My naked body presses to his and the feelings I've come to know so well disappear—for once, I'm free of worry and anxiety.

I SLIDE OUT OF BED, grab my computer from Rian and Dylan's, and return to Knox's apartment without Knox waking. I'd love to stay in bed with him all day, but I'm excited about this new line of girl boss T-shirts I'm working on.

I sit on the recliner with my laptop on my crossed legs and get to work. Well, I try. Because all I can think about is being with Knox in the other room. To be nestled into his chest. To feel his hand slide down my body mindlessly as though he doesn't really know he's doing it.

His phone rings in his room. He probably never put it on silent, as he usually does, since having sex with me threw him off his usual routine. I stand and place my computer on the chair before tiptoeing into his room. I bend over his jeans to grab his phone as it rings over and over. Seriously, when will it go to voicemail?

But before I can get it, a big arm wraps around my waist and tugs me into bed. He pins my back to the mattress and his eyes roam my body. A frown instantly crosses his face. "Why are you dressed?"

I laugh. "Because I slept last night, so I have to work now."

"You can take one day off," he says, his lips falling to my neck. "I wish I was off tonight, but probably a good thing I'm not, otherwise you might not be able to walk tomorrow."

"Is that so?" I wrap my arms around his neck, loving his lips cascading on every inch of my body.

"I'm never going to get enough of you." He takes my hand and slides it down his chest to his hard-on. "See? I already want you again."

"No one said you couldn't have me."

He peeks up as he undresses me. "See, you had to go get dressed and now it's just delaying us."

"I'm just making you work for it."

He throws my leggings on the floor. "I like this going commando thing."

I never did bother to put my panties back on. Maybe I kind of knew we'd end up here again. "I'll remember that."

He stretches, and I kiss his strong shoulders as he grabs a condom from the nightstand. I've never wished I was on the pill or had an IUD more in my life.

As he rests his weight on his heels in front of me while he rolls on the condom, I want to pinch myself that I'm here in bed with him.

"Don't think I've forgotten about the moving thing." He quirks one eyebrow.

"I'm not moving back in."

He shakes his head. "I don't like your stubborn side."

"I guess you have to find something you don't like about me." I laugh because it will be one of many.

"Technically, your stubborn side kind of turns me on." He situates himself between my legs, and without any notice or sign, he thrusts into my wetness. "Damn, you're going to kill me."

I laugh, but then he circles his hips and it's on.

I'm not sure I'll ever get enough of him either. But a girl can try.

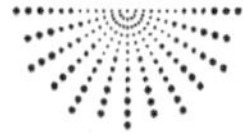

CHAPTER TWENTY-TWO

Knox

I'm in the bathroom, getting ready for work, when I check my phone for the first time since I got off shift. I've been too busy with Kamea to even think of coming up for air.

Huh, Mickey from the old neighborhood hasn't called me in almost a year.

I click the voicemail, walking into my bedroom with just my towel on. Kamea is on the bed with her laptop, working on her new line she says I inspired. I don't know exactly what it is though, since she's keeping it a secret until the first T-shirt comes in.

She's wearing one of my T-shirts right now and it looks damn good on her. The fact that she hasn't pulled away from me since we had sex is making my heart soar, and I have to remind myself it's only been one day. Don't count those paid bills so fast, my mom always says. After she and Dad were able to catch up on bills, one they didn't plan on would arrive in the mailbox the next day.

"Knox, it's Mickey. I saw your girl yesterday. You know, the Polynesian one." As I listen, I look back at Kamea. She must sense my eyes on her because she looks up and smiles. "Anyway, she seemed hard up for money. Said she was trying to catch a train to North Carolina. Something just felt off, so I figured I'd let you know."

I click off the voicemail and fall to my back on the mattress. I turn to look at Kamea as her fingers weave through my wet hair. How different this is than when I was with Leilani. I know I can't compare, but Leilani would've had somewhere to go right after, practically jumping out of bed as soon as we finished the deed. This afterglow thing is nice.

"That was my buddy Mickey. He spotted Leilani last night."

The smile drops from her face for the first time since early this morning. "Oh."

"We could go check it out. You should make her appear in court to get your money, or pay you back," I say.

She shuts her computer *and* that open door I felt with her a moment ago. I have no idea what she's thinking.

"Do you want to find her?" she asks.

I roll over and take her hand. "I want you to get your money back."

"So I can leave?"

I rear my head back. "Not at all."

She shakes her head. "I'm sorry. Just give me a sec." She closes her eyes and massages her temples.

She can't think I still want Leilani, not after this afternoon! But then again, Leilani is like a stubborn splinter in our relationship.

"Hey, you say no and I'm happy to put it on the back

burner," I say. "I mean, eventually a warrant will go out and it'll be my job when I'm on shift to look for her, but not in my free time. I'm doing this solely for you."

She nods. "I want my money, but…"

Fucking shit. Maybe Leilani is more than a splinter.

I slide up the bed and my towel slides off, but I don't care. I kiss Kamea and take her in my arms. "I'm with you. You know that, right?"

She nods, and I inwardly groan as she says, "It's been, like, two minutes."

"It's been weeks, and regardless, I'm over her. Trust me."

"I know I'm being stupid. You don't have to reassure me."

She says that, but I'm thinking I'm going to have to prove it to her in the long run.

"Let's go check it out," she says without making eye contact.

"Tomorrow evening before I head into work?"

"Great." Her tone doesn't match her expression, but I have no choice but to believe that she's okay with this.

If we do find Leilani, I'm going to make sure I don't fuck it up like I did the first time.

"I wish I could bring you to work with me." I kiss her, wishing she could read my mind and know she has nothing to worry about when it comes to Leilani.

"Me too. Or that you were off."

We lie there, and I feel as though the clock is like a bomb about to go off.

"When you get off, I might be at Sweet Infusion with Rian."

I turn so we're facing one another on the bed. "You sure you won't move back in here? I won't make you prepare the coffee." I tuck a strand of her hair behind her ear.

She nods. "I'm positive. Plus, I like the coffee-making

thing. Makes my mind wander and I always get the best ideas for T-shirts when that happens."

I smile and nod. One day I'll get her back in here. "Okay then. I won't pressure you. Yet."

"Yet?" She laughs.

I pull her toward me. "I think we have time for a quickie."

She lifts her phone and shakes her head. "Not if we do it right."

"I've never been late."

She pushes me off her. "And you're not going to be late when you have a promotion on the line either."

I kiss her one more time and get up, knowing how right she is. "Okay, I'm going, but I'm warning you, I might be back on my dinner break."

"I'm sure Patrice would love that." She rolls her eyes and chuckles.

THERE'S no going to see Kamea during dinner because people have lost their damn minds. There must be a full moon.

We're at the station, writing up the paperwork for the thief we apprehended from a house he swears is his parents'. His mom said she's pressing charges, but I can't help but think I'm doing this paperwork for nothing because she'll probably drop the charges.

"So you and Kamea. I saw the kiss." Patrice eyes me over her computer.

"It's nothing."

"That kiss wasn't nothing."

I shake my head to stop her. If I tell her about Kamea and me, she'll continue to torment me for information.

"Fine. Act like that," Patrice says. "I share so much with

you and you're going to act like that with me. Well, whatever. Take that detective position now then."

I blow out a breath at her pouty behavior. Then I think maybe her advice on this whole Leilani and Kamea thing would be good. "Okay, I slept with her."

Her eyes light up and she claps, bouncing in her chair. "I knew it."

"We're together."

"Together?" She claps again like that annoying monkey with the red vest and hat, holding cymbals. "That's great. I really like her. She's so nice, and I can tell she really likes and respects you."

I nod, hoping what she says is the truth. I look around to make sure no one is eavesdropping. "Then I got a call from a buddy of mine in the city. He saw Leilani last night. I mentioned it to Kamea, and she got kind of..."

"Jealous."

I scrunch my eyes. She wasn't fully jealous, just worried.

"And you're surprised?" Patrice asks.

I lean back in my chair. "Well yeah, because we slept together."

A long, annoyed breath falls out of her mouth. "I honestly don't understand how men are so stupid. I mean, what don't you get?"

"What?"

She leans closer. "You picked Leilani over her all those years ago."

"And I explained myself to her. That I was a dick. And I apologized."

"Doesn't take back that you did it. And then Leilani breaks your heart and you go through a list of women to stick your dick in. Then you save Kamea and move her into your place, only to hold her at arm's length until she twists your arm. Of course the girl is a little worried about bringing Leilani back into your life."

"But I told Kamea it's not like that. That I'm with her and happily so."

She rolls her eyes. "Your words don't mean much. It's your actions."

"Well, we haven't even seen Leilani for me to prove it with my actions."

"And when you do, you better be standoffish to her. Don't get that look you usually do. The one when you arrested her."

She's kidding me. "What look is that?"

"The one that shows you still care for the woman."

"I don't care for her." I'm practically grinding my teeth together.

"You scolded me for putting the lights on."

"You forget that I then put on the siren." Patrice is infuriating. Maybe I do want detective, so I don't have to be partners with someone so bossy and opinionated. "I don't want Leilani. I want Kamea."

She smiles and opens her drawer, taking out a Snickers bar. "Good. I wanted to hear you say the words." She bites off the end.

"You're unbelievable."

"I'm just preparing you," she mumbles then swallows. "Because she's going to see things that you don't think are signs. And Leilani is going to use her go-to tactic with you."

"What?"

"Sex. Her body. The fact that you two fucked like rabbits."

She's right, we did, but we never did what I did with Kamea this afternoon. I'm not sure I remember one time Leilani ran her fingers through my hair or looked at me with so much passion. The way my eyes locked with Kamea's when I was inside her. Her lips up my neck and my hands on her ass. The way she opened herself up and let me see who she is inside. It's exactly what I've always wanted and never got with Leilani.

"Let's turn the conversation to you," I say.

But Captain comes by and stands over us, a coffee in his hand. "I hope you two are enjoying this partnership for now because it could be over soon. Interviews are next week and I'm hearing good things about you, Whelan. Don't fuck it up." He sips his coffee and walks away.

Patrice's eyes widen and she smiles. "I guess you'll be done with our bickering in no time, but get that love life of yours solid and situated before you get promoted. Otherwise, I guarantee you, you're bound to fuck it up." She stands and grins at me before heading to the printer.

Detective Whelan. It does have a great ring to it, I must admit.

"You can thank Kamea for giving you an edge." She sits back down and straightens the papers.

"Yeah?"

"She won over a lot of people at Louie's retirement party. Other than DuPont and Milliken thinking she was Leilani, everyone loved her. Felt you two were a great couple."

I tap my pen on my desk. I agree. There's just something about Kamea that feels right. And Patrice is right—I need to make sure Kamea doesn't go anywhere and that I don't scare her off like I did Leilani.

CHAPTER TWENTY-THREE

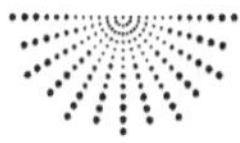

Knox

I get home, and again annoyance flashes through me when I open the door and Kamea isn't at the breakfast bar, on her computer. Silently, I prepare my omelet like most mornings I get off shift. Sitting down on the couch, I turn the television on low so as to not wake Jax. This was my routine before Kamea came into my life, so it shouldn't feel as weird as it does right now.

My gaze roams to her room, and my heart sinks to the bottom of my stomach. But I remind myself that I can't go all caveman and drag her back here. That's how I've lost every other woman I've ever loved. Not that I love Kamea. Not yet anyway. But it would be like me to suffocate her before we got to that part.

I cut my omelet, watching the football highlights on the sports channel.

Jax comes out of his room, heads to the bathroom, and I

roll my eyes when I hear him piss. At least Kamea isn't here to witness it.

"What, Kamea moves out and you stop being our chef? Where's my damn omelet?" Jax plops down on the couch across from me, his gaze traveling to the television.

"Pretty much. I had to act like a good guy to impress her." I smile at him.

"You're a cop. Most people view you as a good guy."

He says that now, but back in the neighborhood when we were punks causing trouble late at night, we didn't think that highly of cops.

"Kamea and I are going to the old neighborhood tonight," I say.

His eyebrows shoot up. "Why?"

"Mickey called. He saw Leilani the other night. I think she might be hanging out at Johnny's. I used to find her there sometimes when we were dating."

"I remember." I doubt he's trying, but if he is, he's not successful at keeping his dislike of Leilani and her disappearing acts to himself. "When are you gonna stop looking for her?"

"Whenever Kamea wants to stop. It's her money we're trying to get."

He nods, but I've known Jax a long time. The look on his face says he doesn't believe it's about Kamea.

"What?" I ask.

He shrugs. "I worry you're about to blow it again."

I sigh. "Blow what?"

"Your chance with Kamea. She's the one for you, yet you still want to fix the one who doesn't want fixing."

I push away my plate and sip my coffee. "I don't want Leilani," I say truthfully.

"Are you sure? Because if you do find her, how do you think it will play out?"

My friends worry about me, which is a great problem to have. Especially when I see a good person like Kamea, who doesn't have nearly the friend circle she should. I'm fortunate to have guys on my side who have been there since the beginning. Although Jax traveled the world for a while, we still kept in contact.

To answer Jax's question, I say, "I'll make sure she either pays Kamea back or gets her ass in for her court date."

"So you'll arrest her again?"

"If she's in the city, it's not my jurisdiction. And she hasn't technically missed her court date."

He nods but holds that smug look, like there's so much more he wants to say.

"Just spit it out."

"Are you finished with that?" He points at my half-eaten omelet.

I slide the plate toward him. "Have at it."

He goes to the kitchen and grabs a new fork before sitting back down across from me. "Listen, I'm not a mind reader, especially when it comes to women. I've never really had a serious relationship, but you and Dylan, you guys were meant for the role of doting husband and adoring father. That's why I don't understand why the two of you can't see when you're about to fuck up a great thing."

"What do you mean? Kamea and I are already together."

He blows out a breath. "Leilani is only going to cause a divide between you and Kamea. One the size of the Grand Canyon. Kamea already feels second best to her. Your relationship is new. It's not going to end well if Leilani makes an appearance."

"I assured Kamea I want her. That I'm over Leilani."

He just chews the omelet.

I'm not sure what people want me to do.

Jax must see my confusion, because he says, "I think it's

inviting the devil into your relationship. Leilani is twisted and conniving, and I've witnessed you fall for her shit too many times."

I stand. "Kamea wants her money sooner than later, and as long as she wants it, or until Leilani misses her court date, we're going to be looking for Leilani."

"Okay," he mumbles over another forkful of omelet. "I'm just doing the shitty job of being your best friend. I have to warn you so I can tell you I told you so later. Good luck."

I walk over to my bedroom door to prepare to shower. "Do you want to come with us?"

"What time? Depends on my appointments at the shop."

Asshole. He and I both know he's going to come. He's just gonna make me work for it.

"Two," I say.

"I'll be there."

TWO O'CLOCK COMES and there's a knock on my bedroom door.

"This is the part where we get out of bed," Kamea says, wiggling in my arms.

But I haven't had enough of her just yet. She sneaked into my bed after her coffee shift and woke me in the best possible way—naked and sucking my cock.

After a round of sex, I fell asleep to her tapping fingers on her keyboard. Although she snuck out of my room at some point because when I woke, she was where I like to see her—at the breakfast bar. Which spurred me to pick her up and take her back into my bedroom.

"Let's go, Whelan, I got shit to do," Jax calls through the door.

Kamea draws back from me. "Why is Jax coming with us?"

I don't want to start our relationship with a lie, but this is for her own good. "He wants to go to the old neighborhood. Plus, he might get more information than I would. Most of them know I'm a cop and Leilani made good friends with a few of them during the time we were together."

She nods. I bring my lips to hers with the hope of getting that look of apprehension off her face. My hand slides down to hers, and I lead her toward my bedroom door. We walk out and I see not only Jax, but Dylan and Rian too.

"What is this, a field trip?" I say.

Kamea's hand falls out of mine and she goes to Rian, asking about the rest of her day at the bakery and saying how she was working all day on T-shirts for the store.

"Excuse me." Jax raises his hand. "Are you pushing Rian's T-shirt order ahead of mine?"

Kamea laughs. "Yours are on their way. Stop worrying."

Sometimes a tinge of jealousy hits me with Jax and Kamea. They formed a friendship so quickly, it scares me that there could be more.

"What exactly are these T-shirts you ordered and am I going to be pissed when you hand them out?" Dylan asks Jax.

"Let's get to the train. I gotta be back for my shift," I say.

We all usher out, but Jax claps Dylan's shoulder and assures Dylan he'll love them. I really need to try to pull that information out of Kamea before Dylan does have a problem on his hands. Sometimes what Jax thinks is funny isn't what everyone else does.

On the train, Kamea sits with me, Rian and Dylan across the aisle, and Jax in front of us. We talk about me playing Santa in two weeks. Jax tells me not to miss it. He's so protective of Jolie, you'd think she was his daughter. Plus Blanca's wedding is fast approaching in the new year, and I have my interview for the detective position in two days. There's a lot of shit going on.

Hopping off the train in our old neighborhood, Dylan clenches Rian's hand a little tighter, not giving her much space to separate. From what I know, he's rarely returned here after Winnie's passing, whereas I have to come visit my parents who still live here.

"Johnny's?" Jax asks.

I nod, and we head in the direction of a dive bar in the middle of the neighborhood. It's a well-known fact that Johnny sells drugs in the back while operating a bar for all the older alcoholics in our neighborhood to drink themselves to oblivion.

Leilani took a liking to Johnny, and him to her, the first time they met at a barbecue I took her too. Although I don't ever hang out at Johnny's Bar, I found her here twice and she wasn't trying to get him to sign a petition to save the whales. She was snorting cocaine. It was my first time finding out she even did that, and in retrospect, it made me want to save her more.

All five of us walk in, and Dylan practically keeps Rian behind him. I'm surprised he even brought her.

Jax walks right up to the bar. The man isn't afraid of shit —not that Dylan or I are. Jax is just more the "let's get this shit handled right the fuck now" kind of guy. He talks to the bartender and the bartender walks away, returning with his finger up, indicating that Johnny will either be out, or we'll be invited into the back.

Kamea's hands tug on mine. As though she can hear my thoughts, she rises up on her tiptoes and whispers, "I don't think you should be here."

"Let's just see if they've seen her and we'll leave."

Jax orders five beers because if we don't, it'll look even more suspicious. We situate ourselves at a table in the corner, and I take the chair against the wall with Kamea on my left. This way I have eyes everywhere.

Johnny walks out looking as though he's aged ten years since I saw him last—which wasn't that long ago. He nods to Jax and laughs, finding me at the table.

"I didn't know the entire gang was here." Johnny slaps handshakes and pulls us in for hugs. He does a double-take on Kamea, and I make sure he sees my hand in hers. He chuckles. "To what do I owe this visit?"

"We're looking for Leilani," Jax says. "Heard she was around here a few days ago."

"Leilani?" He acts as if he doesn't remember her. Bullshit.

"You know… Knox's ex."

Kamea's hand goes limp in mine, but I squeeze hers harder.

"Sorry, I haven't seen her in years. The Polynesian one, right?" He eyes Kamea.

She leans in closer to me.

"Yes. Think hard, Johnny," Jax says.

"Look at this girl, Phillips, she's yours?" He doesn't answer but moves the conversation to Dylan.

"Yeah, she's mine."

Johnny exaggerates a look up and down Rian that makes my skin crawl. I can't imagine how Dylan's feeling.

"Yeah, we're out. We're going for a walk." Dylan stands and waits for Rian to join him. "Keep livin' the dream, Johnny."

They walk out, and Johnny sits at the table. "Listen." He looks around as if he's going to give us some top-secret information. "I don't know where she is. She was here a few days ago, mostly just as a reference for someone. Said the guy could be trusted."

I nod, understanding that she vouched for someone to be

either a dealer or a buyer. Good to know she's on the straight and narrow.

"But that's all I got," he says.

"Who was the guy?" Kamea asks.

Johnny smiles at her, glancing at her breasts then back at her eyes. "Some Wade guy."

Kamea hits me. "That's one of them."

"One of who?" Johnny asks.

Jax leans back and sips his beer. His presence alone intimidates people, mostly because once upon a time he couldn't control his temper. "One of the douchebags who got her kicked out of her apartment."

Johnny nods. "That sucks. Is that why you want Leilani? Are you her sister or something?"

"No!" Kamea rolls her eyes. "She owes me money."

"She has a court date coming up quick. If she doesn't show, she'll have a warrant issued for her arrest. And you know who will start sniffing around then…" I lay out the information.

Johnny nods.

So long, Wade and Leilani, Johnny is done with you now.

The door of the bar opens again. I expect to find Dylan and Rian telling us it's time to go, but it's not either of them.

"Knox Michael Whelan, you come to this neighborhood and you don't come to see me?"

"Who's that?" Kamea whispers.

Jax laughs hard and slaps the table. He stands and beelines right over to her. "Momma Whelan!"

Fuck me.

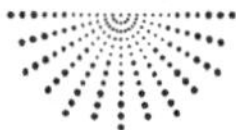

CHAPTER TWENTY-FOUR

Knox

My mom hugs Jax as though he's her son too. After Jax separates from her, she stands there with her eyebrows raised at me. Want to see a grown man cower? Bring his mom.

"Hey, Mom," I say, rising from the chair and waiting for Kamea to come with me.

My mom's eyes zero in our linked hands and she glances to Jax for confirmation.

He nods and puts his arm around her shoulders. "Our boy has a girlfriend." He pretends as though he's going to cry.

I swear I could punch him in the gut. Instead I give my mom a short hug. She's too preoccupied with finding out who Kamea is to me to care about it though.

"This is Kamea, my girlfriend." I mean, she is. We never said we were monogamous, nor have we been together that long, but it feels implied to me. I hope it's okay that I referred to her as that.

Kamea holds out her hand to my mom. "Hi, Mrs. Whelan, it's nice to meet you."

I slide my arm around Kamea's waist and tuck her against my side.

My mom shakes her hand. "Peggy, please. It's nice to meet you." Mom looks around the bar. "Johnny."

"Hey, Mrs. Whelan."

"You need to clean up this bar." She scans the area, her lips straightening as she takes in more men slumped over on the bar top.

"Yes, ma'am." Johnny is such a kiss-ass. He fooled a lot of parents growing up, but never my mom.

"Come on, everyone, you're coming to our house so I can feed you." Mom ushers us all outside.

"Awesome." Jax fist-pumps. "This trip just became worth it."

"Bye, Johnny," I say. "Thanks for the… beer."

He nods. We both know this bar is a dead-end to finding Leilani, and part of me feels at this point, we need to stop looking for her.

Walking out of the bar, I shouldn't be—but I am—surprised to see my dad talking to Dylan and Rian. He's going on and on about the neighborhood and how this place isn't making it any better. Says how smart we all were to move to Cliffton Heights. I wish they would've followed me, but their jobs are here.

"So, sweetie, tell me about yourself." My mom links her arm through Kamea's and walks ahead with her.

Kamea gives me a fleeting look over her shoulder, but she's safe with my mom.

"Son, why the hell are you hanging around that bar?" Dad puts one arm around me, pulling me into his body. Since he's about the same height as me and bigger in width now that he's got more of a desk job, I feel like a kid for the first time in a long time.

"Just looking for someone."

He stops and lets the others walk ahead. "Again?"

I love my friends and they've all been there for me, but it's my dad who knows every facet of my relationship with Leilani. He said he'd never tell my mom, but I can't say for sure that he's kept everything to himself. But he's my confidant.

I glance up before lowering my voice. "Kamea bailed her out and now it looks like she might skip out on bail. Kamea needs to get the money."

He nods. "I thought she was out of your life?"

"So did I," I say.

"So Kamea is friends with Leilani?"

I nod.

"Why can't you just find a no-drama girlfriend? I swear." He slaps me on the back.

I'm with him—why can't my love life be drama free?

We walk a few feet in silence.

"She's very pretty though. You really like her?" he asks.

"I do."

"Good."

All my dad wants is for me to be happy. My mom too, but she can be judgmental. She never liked my college girlfriend, nor did she like Leilani. My mom has a certain vision of the woman I should end up with and neither of them were it. I'm not sure she'll be happy no matter who I choose.

We walk toward my parents' two-bedroom apartment. My mom uses her key to open the door for the building, and we walk up the stained linoleum steps. Part of me is ashamed that Kamea will see how poor my parents are. I grew up without any money, but I was still seen as fortunate because I had two parents. Hell, Dylan and Jax didn't even have one. They had a foster mom.

My mom is asking them if they like galumpkis while she inserts the key into their apartment door.

"Mom, Kamea is a vegetarian." The last thing she wants to eat is cabbage leaves stuffed with ground meat and rice.

"Oh. Well, that's very environmentally-friendly of you."

I shake my head because my mom just doesn't get it. My dad smacks me over the head for embarrassing my mother.

Kamea glances at me. "It's fine, I'm not hungry."

"Nonsense, everyone eats at the Whelans'. I'm sure I have vegetables. But you are going to challenge me." Mom laughs as we file into my parents' apartment.

Jax falls onto the couch and grabs the remote. My dad kicks Jax's legs to get his feet off the coffee table and takes the remote from his hand.

"You didn't warp back to being sixteen, Jax." Dad sits in his armchair and pulls back the recliner to rest his feet.

Jax groans. "You're still watching black and white movies."

Rian sits at the kitchen table with Kamea on her right. Dylan sits down next to Jax, talking to my dad about the neighborhood and if he thinks things will ever turn around. I head into the kitchen with my mom. Her head is buried in the cupboard as the oven warms up.

"You don't have to feed us, Mom. We were going to go out to eat. I'm on shift tonight."

She peeks her head out of the cupboard and looks at the clock. "You have plenty of time. I can't believe you'd come down here and not see us. Thankfully Dylan spotted us across the street of that dingy bar you were in."

"Yeah, I'll need to thank him for that later."

She peeks her head out again and shoots me a death stare. "So tell me about her."

"There's not much to tell."

She pulls out a box of crackers. "Cheese isn't vegetarian, right?" She opens the fridge.

"That's vegan. She'll eat cheese."

"And salami. I have cheese and salami." Her smile is so wide, I hate to disappoint her.

"Salami is meat, Mom."

Her head falls back. "Yes, of course. Okay." She walks away from me and says to Kamea, "I've got crackers and cheese. What about olives? Do you like olives? Tim loves them."

Without Kamea answering, my mom returns to our small galley kitchen. The buzzer of the oven goes off and she takes the galumpkis out of the fridge and places them into the oven before setting a timer. Mom takes out a jar of black olives and puts them in a bowl, then sets them in front of Kamea.

"Mom, relax." I put my hand over hers. "You don't have to entertain us. You didn't even know we were coming."

"And whose fault is that?" She pokes me in the chest.

I wrap her up in a hug. "It's new," I whisper. "I don't want to scare her."

Mom draws back and puts her hands on my cheeks. "You worry too much. Any woman would be lucky to have you. You know your dad sat outside my apartment building for two days, asking me out every time I left. Grandpa wanted Uncle Mark to make him leave. If they like you, they don't see your love as smothering. You just pick the wrong girls." She pats my cheek.

I nod because it's the same thing she's always told me.

"Go get to know her. I've got this." I push Mom toward the table with Kamea and Rian.

She smiles, and after everyone has a drink in their hands, Mom sits down with the girls. I busy myself in the kitchen, trying to find something Kamea will actually enjoy. Then I have the idea to order Chinese food so my mom can have a night of enjoyment too.

Heading into my old childhood room, I call up and order the Chinese food, but before I can head back into the living room, Kamea walks in.

"This is your childhood bedroom?" she asks.

"I thought you were talking to my mom," I say, sitting on my bed.

"Someone called." She sits next to me on my twin bed, her eyes scanning the area. "It's nice."

"It's small," I say.

She shrugs, eyeing my bookcase. "Trophies from football?"

"Yeah."

"You okay?" She tilts her head. "You seem tense."

I drag her onto my lap and she winds her arms around my neck. I kiss her. "I'm great right now."

"So… Leilani was using?"

I figured she'd ask at some point. I nod. "I found her twice, but I don't think it was a regular thing."

"That's good." Her head falls to my shoulder and she suddenly looks exhausted.

I kiss her forehead, annoyed and happy that we're at my parents'. "I ordered you some food. We need to keep your energy up."

She giggles. "I like your parents. They seem nice."

"They're good people."

"Your mom wants to come to Cliffton Heights and have Rian's pastries and my coffee. And she wants me to design shirts for her knitting club."

I laugh.

"And she said I'm to come for Thanksgiving dinner. That you usually volunteer first then have dinner?"

I nod. "You don't have to come."

"I want to."

"Why?"

She sits up a little straighter and looks me in the eye. "They're important to you, so they're important to me. I want to have a relationship. Plus I told your mom I'll teach her how to make a tofu turkey."

I gape. "Tofu?" My dad would die.

She giggles. "Come on, a little tofu never hurt anyone."

I toss her onto her back on the bed and crawl on top of her, wishing I could shut that door and have sex with her. She keeps laughing.

"What's so funny?"

"I wish I could've kept it a secret until Thanksgiving and placed a tofu turkey in front of you, just to see your face."

I tickle her. "You think that's funny?"

She wiggles and squirms and my dick grows hard. "I do."

As though I have no control, my lips find hers and I kiss her, my tongue sliding into her mouth. She moans, and one leg wraps around my leg, allowing me to grind into her.

"*Knox!*" my mom yells.

I scramble off Kamea as though I'm in high school and my parents just got home. I wipe my mouth as Kamea laughs, getting up from the bed to pretend she's looking at trophies. I fix my pants so my hard-on isn't on display for my mom.

Mom comes to the doorway. "You didn't order Chinese food, did you?"

I nod. "I did."

She smiles in appreciation, then she looks to where Kamea is. "Has Knox told you what a great football player he was?"

Kamea listens to my mom brag about me and my accomplishments. Every once in a while, Kamea's gaze shoots to me and she looks as though she wishes she could pounce on me.

I wish the same thing. But mostly she listens to my mom, asking questions and giving her the respect she deserves just for being my mom. My mom keeps touching Kamea's arm, and Kamea never steps away. She laughs with my mom and my heart feels as if it's growing as I watch the two of them together.

Maybe she is the one after all.

CHAPTER TWENTY-FIVE

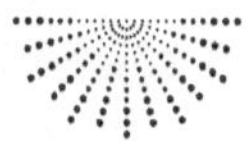

Kamea

It's the night before Thanksgiving and everyone has decided to head to the bar. Knox got the holiday off, so instead of being home this weekend, he's off tonight and tomorrow. But since Jax and Dylan have to work, the girls decided we'd go to the bar first and the guys could catch up.

We Uber down to the riverfront of Cliffton Heights, where a lot of the clubs and bars are located.

When we exit the two cars, Sierra's arm swings through mine. "I really like you. You're perfect for him and you fit in perfectly with us."

I chuckle. "Thank you."

She has no idea how much her words mean to me. Ever since leaving North Carolina, I haven't had friends I could depend on. It's crazy to feel that these women have my back after only a few weeks, but Rian allowed me to move in when it's clear Dylan isn't happy about it, and Sierra let me borrow her dress, Blanca did my makeup. And Evan is always asking me how my day was. Finally, after all this time, I feel as though I fit somewhere. I'm aware that has a lot to do with Knox though. And if Knox and I go south, all this might disappear too.

We walk into the bar. The music is on, but it isn't pounding bass. Blanca says something to the bartender and he nods, pointing toward a table in the corner that's big enough for all of us. She waves us over and we all get seated, taking off our coats and hanging our purses off the back of the chairs. The waitress appears immediately and we all order our drinks.

"So spill it," Blanca says to me.

"Spill what?" I ask.

"You and Knox. You're officially together?"

I nod, feeling heat rush to my cheeks. I'm not sure why I'm embarrassed. Being with him is the best feeling in the world. He's so open with his thoughts and feelings, I have no idea how Leilani didn't fall head over heels for him. Then again, he definitely has a sense of commitment that most likely scared her.

"*Yay!*" Blanca claps. "We should order champagne."

"I heard you really nailed it by moving in with Rian." Sierra elbows me. "Totally something I would've done. When you know, you know, right?"

I nod, although I don't think I'm nearly the hard-ass Sierra is. With her perfect style and confidence, she still intimidates me a little.

"What's everyone doing for Thanksgiving?" I ask to get the heat off of me. I'm afraid I could jinx us if I talk too much about Knox and me.

"We're going to my dad's, but then we're heading to the shelter to see Knox as Santa." Sierra sips her drink.

"My parents' house with my brothers and their wives, but we're catching a ride with Sierra and Adrian over to the shelter too," Blanca says.

"We're at Seth's parents and we're hoping to get over to Rian's for dessert, then the shelter," Evan says.

"You're stuck with us the entire day," Rian says to me.

"I'm sure Dylan isn't too happy about that," I say.

Sierra's head whips toward Rian. "What am I missing?"

Rian's lips tipping down is her way of apology, but it's not her fault that Dylan has a problem with me. "He's just being Dylan."

"You mean the way he was with—"

Rian nods before Sierra can finish.

"What am I missing?" I ask since the conversation took a turn into the dark for me.

"Dylan is protective over Knox. Kind of like a big brother," Rian says. "He's worried because you were friends with Leilani, that you two could have some scheme going."

My eyes widen, and I feel sick to my stomach. "What?"

"He's insane." Blanca rolls her eyes.

Rian nods. "He is. I told him that, but the three of them..." She looks at me. "Jax, Dylan, and Knox have been friends since childhood and I think they just look out for one another. Some kind of bro code."

"Funny, since when Jax returned, Dylan wasn't happy." Sierra rolls her eyes.

I suddenly feel so lost in this group dynamic. "I'm going to head to the bathroom."

"I'll go with you," Evan says.

"Kamea," Rian calls.

I turn back around. She doesn't need to feel guilty for communicating what her fiancé thinks. "It's okay. I get his apprehension. He's a good friend to Knox and that's what matters. Honestly."

Her shoulders sink, but I turn to head to the bathroom. Evan's hot on my heels as we weave through the over-crowded bar toward the bathroom. When I enter, I stare at myself in the mirror, pushing away the negative thoughts Dylan has about me. I just have to prove to him that I'm not Leilani, that I care for Knox, and that I'm not going to run away. While I use the bathroom, I try to think of some way to get on Dylan's good side. How can I prove to him that he can trust me?

I exit the stall, and Evan sighs when she sees me. Then she buckles over in laughter. "You're never going to believe what just happened to me."

"What?" I wash my hands, staring at her through the mirror.

"A group got between us and I couldn't see you anymore. Then I put my arm through this girl's arm, thinking it was you. I was laughing and telling her how crazy the bar is and how you don't have to worry about Dylan. But when she didn't answer, I finally looked at her and it wasn't you. I swear she's your doppelgänger from behind." She laughs. "I don't think she appreciated it because she yanked her arm out of mine and gave me a dirty look."

I laugh, drying my hands. "Sorry, I just wanted to get away from the table for a second. Clear my head."

She leans her hip on the counter. "Listen. I've only been in this group for a short time, but they really have been great friends to me. From what Seth says, Leilani took a sledge-hammer to Knox."

I hold up my hand. "I've heard it all, and honestly, I'm done hearing it. Knox loved Leilani. Great. I get it."

She runs her hand along my upper arm. "I didn't mean that."

I look away from her, sick and tired of feeling second best

every time Leilani's damn name comes up. When will she not be this invisible third wheel in our relationship?

"I see the way he looks at you. He's fixated on you when we're all together."

And when I'm with Knox, I never think about Leilani. I never doubt his feelings for me. But times like now, when someone puts me in the same boat as Leilani, or when I have to hear for the millionth time how crushed he was when she left, I feel the doubts and questions of whether I'm the rebound or a replacement.

"It's fine, really. I'm just being silly." I wave it off.

"Seth says he's never seen him so happy."

"Thanks, Evan. I'm going to go back. I don't want Rian to think I'm mad."

"Come on. Let's just enjoy tonight." Evan opens the door, and we step out into the hallway for the bathrooms. We're about to go single file through the crowd when Evan's hand lands on my arm. "That's her. I don't see the resemblance face to face, but from behind, I can see why I thought it. I'll have to pay more attention to what you're wearing from now on."

Evan's too busy laughing to notice that the girl she thought was me is staring at me and I at her. Because the girl she thought was me is Leilani.

Leilani walks toward me, her beer hanging in her fingers at her side. She's wearing black leather pants and a black shirt that dips down past her cleavage. The entire outfit shows off her body, and guys check her out as she walks by them.

"Kamea!" she exclaims as she gets closer, setting her beer on a nearby table before pulling me in for a hug. Just as forcefully as she pulled me in, she pushes me away.

"You know her?" Evan asks me, pointing at Leilani.

"Evan, this is Leilani. Leilani, this is Evan."

Leilani finally stops looking at me and shifts her attention to Evan. "Seth's girl, right?"

"Um… yeah."

"Knox always told me he had a thing for you. It wasn't hard to put it together when you thought I was Kamea. People have always mistaken us, right, Kam?" She puts her arm around me. "The Polynesian genes are strong, I guess."

She's being friendly, and I fear this is a calm before the storm.

"So you guys are friends?" Leilani asks, glancing over her shoulder at the other girls at our table—they're enthralled in a conversation and don't see what's happening. "You're friends with all of Knox's friends? How'd that happen?"

"Well…" Evan puts her hands on her hips, head swiveling as though she's ready to tell Kamea off. "When you skipped on the bail that Kamea paid—"

I place my hand on Evan's arm to stop her from doing what I need to do. "The truth is, after your friends got me kicked out of my apartment and you ran off with them, Knox found me under an overpass and gave me a place to sleep. We've been all over trying to find you, Leilani. I told you I needed that bail money."

Leilani rolls her eyes. "An overpass? Seriously, Kamea? You didn't have anywhere else to go? So dramatic."

"She didn't. No one would choose to sleep—"

Again I put my hand on Evan's arm, and when she looks over to me, I shake my head. Leilani's not worth it.

"So now you're friends with all of them?" There's jealousy in Leilani's tone, and I remember she was never really welcomed into the group—or, as usual, she chose to distance herself.

"I am." I nod.

She blows out a breath. "They're not real friends."

"And you are?" Evan screams.

Leilani shakes her head before looking at me.

"And you are?" I repeat Evan's words. "You didn't care about me or what I'm trying to accomplish. I told you I needed the money and you took off. What kind of friend are you?"

"You don't want to go there." Leilani's words hold a threat.

I throw my hands in the air. "Oh my God, just say it."

"You wouldn't even come with me. You just said you couldn't."

I toss back my head. "Because I wasn't going to be a seventeen-year-old runaway. And you didn't have to leave."

"Yes, I did. Because I saved you. I had to leave because I saved you and my life was hell after that."

Here we go. "Well, you know what? Don't pay me the money back early then. Whatever. We're even either way, okay?"

"I was going to pay you back," Leilani says.

"Right. That's why you disappeared and wouldn't answer my calls. Well, you're off the hook. So, show up or don't to the court date, that's your decision. I hope you do so I can get my money back and so that you can face this and then move on but I will no longer feel guilty for your poor decisions."

She puts her hands on her hips and stares at me. "That's how you're going to play this?"

"Yes. I don't want to be friends with you anymore, Leilani. You don't care about anyone but yourself."

Evan stands there, her head flying back and forth between us, trying to keep up.

"You've always been my girl," Leilani says with a note of sadness to her voice.

"Only when you needed me. Whenever I need you, I'm hung out to dry. Bye, Leilani." I slide past her.

Evan quickly follows me. The farther away I get from

Leilani, the more weight lifts off me. I should've done that years ago.

When two arms wrap around my waist and a scratchy cheek runs along my neck, I close my eyes.

"Hey, beautiful," Knox whispers in my ear, lowering my feet back onto the floor. I turn around in his arms, and his smile dims instantly. "What's wrong?"

"Leilani is here," I say.

His hands leave my body and he scans the area. I'm not sure if he spots her or not, but then he's gone, winding through people, searching for her. My heart sinks into my stomach as I watch him frantically looking for her, watering that seed of doubt inside me. Is Knox really over Leilani?

CHAPTER TWENTY-SIX

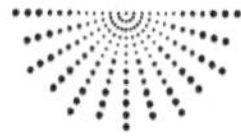

Knox

After searching the entire bar, I question whether Kamea really saw Leilani. How could she vanish that quickly? Returning to the table, I take the chair next to Kamea. Thankfully, the conversation is on Blanca and Ethan's wedding, and since they're all distracted, I can ask Kamea what happened.

"When did you see her?"

She sips her drink. "A minute or so before you wrapped your arms around me."

I note that she's not looking directly at me. "And what did she say?"

She shrugs. "Just that these girls aren't real friends. Made me feel like shit about her running away in high school and me not going with her." Her eyes flicker across the table. "Evan heard everything."

I glance over my shoulder where Evan seems to be recounting the entire conversation to Seth. He shoots me a look to say "fuck, man."

My thoughts exactly. Because if it was only a minute before I arrived, that means Leilani now knows I'm with Kamea. And although I don't give a shit what Leilani thinks, it could be why Kamea is presently a damn ice sculpture.

"I told her to keep the money and we're even." Kamea sucks back a large part of her drink.

"You what?" I yell. The group looks at me, so I lower my voice. "Why would you do that?"

"Because I don't care about the money. All I care about is that she's out of my life."

I reach for her hand and she allows me to hold it, but even after I squeeze it, it lays limp. "True. That's true. We want her out of our life." I slide closer and kiss her cheek.

"I do, but do you?" she asks.

"Hey. Come with me." I stand and tug her up by her hand. "Grab your jacket." I look at our group. "We'll be back."

They all nod as if they weren't eavesdropping.

I never let Kamea go as I guide us out of the crowded bar. Once we're by the riverfront, I lead us down the path away from the bar, hoping like hell Leilani doesn't show up. If I'm going to make progress with Kamea, I need Leilani far, far away.

"You ran after her," Kamea says before I have a chance to say anything.

"Because we've been looking for her. You need your money."

"Your face. Your eyes. You wanted to see her." She sits on a bench as though she doesn't have the energy to continue on.

"I don't want her. I only went after her because she owed you money and I was going to get it back for you."

Her stiff body language says she doesn't believe me, and I have no idea how to convince her. I fist my hands at my sides.

Kamea says, "I've never had the self-confidence I should, but being with you, it was growing. But every time her name comes up or I have to hear how heartbroken you were over her, all those doubts creep in." She stands and goes to the concrete ledge that overlooks the river.

I follow and place my hand on her back. Leilani fucked with my life long enough. I'm not going to allow her to fuck this up for me. "I like you. I'm with you."

"Out of default?" She looks at me for a moment before looking back at the river.

"How could you think that? I wasn't planning on falling for you. But everything about you—"

"Is it because I look like her?" she spits out before I can finish.

"God, no. And you don't, by the way. You don't look like her at all. But if you have to know"—she opens her mouth and I put my finger to her lips with the hopes she doesn't snap it away—"let me finish this."

She nods.

"I fell for the woman you are in here." I place my hand over her heart. "Don't get me wrong, you're beautiful, gorgeous face, a total knockout, but it's the way you are with people. Your kindness. The fact that you've allowed my friends to bombard their way into your life. How you let me snuggle close to you when we sleep. The way you run your fingers through my hair and down my cheeks. That you ask me how my day was and actually remember the things I told you. How you were ready to let my mom feed you olives and cheese and act like it's a damn meal."

She smiles and I think that I might almost have her. "God, Kamea, I'm not with you as a default. I'm with you because I should've always been you. From the beginning, I should've gone home with you. It's not you being compared to Leilani. Leilani doesn't hold a candle up to you."

I place my hands on her hips and swivel her to face me. "I don't want to scare you, but I've fallen for you. You're everything I've been looking for. I think we have something really special."

Her smile grows.

"Tell me you feel this too," I say. "That it's different than anything else you've ever experienced. That you fit perfectly alongside me. You feel it, right?"

She nods.

"Then believe in it and in me. Trust me." I tug her toward me, and her hands fall to my chest. I place a hand on her cheek, and she tilts her face into my palm. "I never want you to feel second best."

I lower my head and my lips meet hers. She rises up on her tiptoes, so I don't have to strain too far down. Our tongues tangle and slide in the dance we've come to know.

Once it's over, she draws back. "I'm sorry. I hate that I allow her to make me feel less than."

"Ask me any time and I'll reassure you about how magnificent you are."

She sighs and her forehead falls to my chest.

"Now let's go have fun with our friends."

She steps back as I take her hand. "They're your friends."

"I don't think so. Everyone at the table was looking at me like I was a moron for making you sad. Believe me, they're your friends too."

I hope she believes me. We're in a weird situation, and I wish everyone would stop telling her what a mess I was when Leilani left. That only increases her anxiety and mistrust of what's developing between us. I just need to make sure I'm extra attentive, so she knows my feelings for her aren't even in the same realm of what I felt for Leilani. I mean hell, I haven't fucked Kamea in a public area once. Doesn't she realize that says it all?

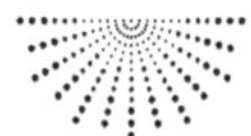

CHAPTER TWENTY-SEVEN

Kamea

nox comes out of the shower. He had his detective interview yesterday, and now we wait until all the applicants have been interviewed to see if there's another round.

Today is Thanksgiving, and other than a text from my brother, I haven't heard from my family. I assume my parents are still upset I decided to move away.

Even though we've had sex too many times to count, my boyfriend wearing just a towel still makes me vibrate with want. I can't believe I allowed my insecurity over Leilani to show last night at the bar. Although Knox says I can talk to him about it, I can't nag him to delve into how much he cares for me every time I feel the slightest bit worried about his feelings toward me.

"What are you thinking about?" He goes to his closet.

I place my computer on the bed. "That I wish we could eat Thanksgiving dinner in the bed, alone."

He glances over his shoulder. "Me too. Believe me, I'm just thankful I'm off. After the entire Santa thing is over, we're out of there."

I can't wait to see him play Santa for Jolie's grandmother's shelter. Since Knox's parents always go to a different shelter to volunteer on Thanksgiving, they're going to visit us there after they're done. Then we're eating at Rian and Dylan's.

When he turns around to place his pants and shirt on the mattress, I slide down the bed. Placing my hands on his hips, I pull him to me.

One of his hands threads through my hair while the other one tips my face up to his. "What are you doing?"

I run my hand along the bulge under his towel and apply pressure. He groans and his fingers tighten in my strands.

"What do you think I'm doing?"

I unhook his towel and it falls to the floor. His dick is right in front of me, pointing north. I grip the base of his cock and leave my eyes on his while I lick up his length, then cover the tip with my mouth and suck.

"Hell, Kamea," he says and rocks into my mouth.

I've only gone down on him before we have sex and never until he came in my mouth, but today is the day. I won't allow him to deter me away. Unfortunately, I don't have a lot of experience, but he's never complained before.

I tighten my grip over his shaft and pump at the same pace as I do with my mouth.

The hand that was on my chin slides down the front of my T-shirt until he takes my bare breast and his thumb and forefinger pinch my nipple. "It feels so good."

He rocks into my mouth. I keep a loose enough grip to move up and down, but I know he likes it firm. I bob my head at the same pace as my hand, but it isn't until I use my free hand to cup his balls that he loses all control.

"Let's fuck, so you can get my cock inside you."

I shake my head, continuing to take him in and out of my mouth. And then I do something I've only ever seen in porn —I open my mouth all the way until the tip of his dick hits the back of my throat.

His hips retract back as if the pleasure is too much to take, then he thrusts inside my mouth again as if he misses it.

"I'm coming," he says.

His fingers grip my hair so tight the pain/pleasure mix only makes me want to continue, so I don't stop. He pumps into me then stills, his eyes falling closed. I've never felt so powerful. That might sound crazy, but the fact I got him so hot and horny he could barely control himself is satisfying not just to him, but to me.

I swallow, and his hands loosen in my hair, his finger sliding down my jawline until he cups my chin and turns it up toward him. "That was amazing. Today I'm thankful for blowjobs from my hot girlfriend."

I laugh and he bends down, claiming my lips as he slides me back on the bed. "Oh no, we don't have that much time."

He tears off my pajama shorts and throws them across the room, nestling between my legs. From the first lick, I give up the fight.

We leave for the shelter ten minutes late, but sometimes Santa has to make sure the missus is taken care of first.

WE ARRIVE at the shelter and Frankie ushers Knox through the back door. "Kamea, you can go through the front. Jolie and my mom are there. I have to get the big guy ready since he's late."

Frankie has that mom look only real moms can pull off. The one that makes even a cop twice her size wince.

"Good luck." I give him two thumbs up.

Walking into the shelter area, I find Jax already there with Jolie and Sandy.

"What's up? Better mood since last night?" Jax asks.

Sandy hugs me, and I put on an apron and wash my hands to help pass out candy canes to the guests. Our job is to get the kids excited about Santa's arrival.

"I'm fine," I say.

"Yeah? Were those screams last night all the insecurity toward Leilani being let out of you?"

I hate that Jax sees and knows everything. He probably pegged this would happen. "I'm not proud of my insecurities, okay?"

He twirls his finger, and I circle around for him to tie my apron in the back.

I add, "It's embarrassing."

"Yeah, needy girls are the worst."

I turn back around when he's done, and my shoulders sink. "Thanks for making me feel better."

"I'm just saying, you're going to have to get over it." He shrugs.

"Yeah, I get it."

I walk away from Jax, not into having this conversation with him. I already feel stupid and immature. He passes around coloring books, and Jolie follows him with crayons.

A few minutes later, Jax is back at my side. "I didn't mean to make you feel bad. I get it. Do you think guys don't have insecurities?"

I huff, rolling my eyes at him.

He holds up his hand. "We do. Swear it. We doubt ourselves. Guys just hide it better. Like last night, I probably would have punched Leilani."

"I'm not a physical person."

"Mommy says no hitting," Jolie says from behind us. I forget too often that she's always listening.

"If someone hits you first, you hit back," Jax says.

I stop and circle around. "No, Jolie, you do not. You listen to your mommy."

Jolie nods, but she's kind of badass like her mom. I have a feeling she might hit first.

"It's cool though, you gotta get that shit out," Jax says. "Just don't make it a habit."

I pass out four candy canes to a family at one of the tables. "I don't remember asking you for your opinion."

He laughs. "Since when do I wait for people to ask?"

"Never."

"Exactly. Be more like me."

I get that Jax is trying to be nice and, in his own special way, make me feel better, but I'm not one hundred percent sure Leilani *is* out of Knox's mind. Ugh, I hate admitting that even to myself.

"Kamea!"

I look up to find Peggy, Knox's mom, and his dad walking in with a big bag full of gifts.

I step aside so we don't interrupt the guests from their Thanksgiving meal. "Hi, Mr. and Mrs. Whelan."

She playfully slaps me on the shoulder. "Nonsense. Peggy and Tim, remember?"

I nod, but I don't feel comfortable calling them by their first names.

"These are the gifts. Each one marked with an age and gender." Tim holds the bag out to Jax.

"I'll take them back," Jax says.

"That was kind of you," I say.

Peggy shrugs. "I don't come to a shelter without gifts. I

figure…" She stops when she spots Jolie between us. "You're a cutie."

"Jolie." She holds out her hand. "Why are you bringing gifts?"

"For the children in a few weeks…" Her words trail off when she realizes Jolie probably still believes in Santa.

Between this and at Ink Envy the other day, Santa's secret is gonna be blown.

"Santa brings the gifts," Jolie says.

"Yes, but sometimes he asks me to bring extras," Peggy says.

Jolie's eyes widen. "You know Santa?"

"Well, me and the missus were friends back in high school."

How on Earth Peggy keeps up this show, I have no idea. She was probably an amazing mom because she can really think on her feet.

"I gotta go tell my mom! Can you get a letter up to Santa?" Jolie asks, practically vibrating.

Peggy nods. "Sure thing."

Jolie runs away and into the back, where Knox is getting dressed.

"You just made her day," I say.

"I'll give the letter to her mom. Come on, I'll help you."

Peggy takes the candy canes and passes them out while Tim does the coloring books and crayons. Jolie returns, and Peggy puts the letter in her purse while Jolie goes back to dishing out crayons to the young kids. Tim is so great with her, I can't help but think what great grandparents they'll be someday. Which only pulls me back into my thoughts of my own parents. The odd time I do call home they either don't answer or they do and it's just a stilted one-sided conversation on my part. All because I chose to leave, they're never going to meet their grandchildren. How stubborn can they be?

Once everything is passed out and almost all of our friends have arrived, Knox comes out in the Santa suit.

I take a seat next to Peggy.

"Look at him," she says. "Smile, Santa!"

Knox looks up and fakes a smile, but as soon as a kid hops up on his lap, he does in fact smile. He talks with each child for a few minutes, then Frankie, who's dressed as an elf, helps them back to their parents and gives them a letter and crayon to write their letter since Santa's memory fails him sometimes.

"Where are your parents?" Peggy asks me when about half the kids have had their visit with Santa.

My throat dries up. Surely a woman who takes in her son's friends won't understand why I no longer speak to my parents. "They're in North Carolina."

"Oh, and you didn't want to go home to celebrate the holiday? I guess it's a short one. Will you be with them for Christmas?"

Just rip off the damn Band-Aid, Kamea. "I don't really talk to my parents."

"Oh." She's silent for a moment. "Reminds me of Leilani. She didn't either."

So she's been in this situation with Leilani before. Great. That's really helping the pit in my stomach.

"Yeah, we were friends," I say.

"I know. Knox told me."

I look at her with shock. "He did?"

"Yeah. We don't have a lot of secrets." She shrugs. "Why don't you talk to your parents?"

I pick at the edge of a leftover coloring book. "I left after high school. They didn't want me to go, so we don't talk."

"That's sad." Her hand falls to my back and she rubs it up

and down. "Such a silly reason to not have your kid in your life."

Preach, Peggy. Preach.

"It's them missing out. Maybe they'll come around. Sometimes a wedding will bring a family together." She winks.

I laugh. "You aren't suggesting…"

She giggles and points at Knox, who is staring at us. "Well, I've never seen my son more in love with someone than he is with you. A mother knows."

I smile and Knox's grows wider. Who would've guessed it'd be Knox's mom to finally make me feel better?

CHAPTER TWENTY-EIGHT

Knox

After our roll call, Cap says, "Stay back, Whelan."

I haven't heard anything in the past week about the interviews for detective, and I keep thinking they're going to ask us to interview a second time. "Yes, Captain?"

Patrice heads out, giving DuPont crap about his wife getting pregnant for the fifth time and asking whether he's sure they're all his because they're way too cute to have his DNA. Cap glances at the door, waiting for everyone to leave. I'm not sure if that's good or bad.

"Ben, shut the door," he says, and Ben does shut the door.

The poor guy had some reprieve until the retirement party. Now I no longer get hell since I'm dating Kamea. Kind of amazing how right Cap was with that move. But that leaves Ben as the butt of every joke once again.

"Leilani's court date is tomorrow morning," Cap says. "If she doesn't show up at nine o'clock, a warrant will be issued.

I just want to make sure you're okay arresting her if you see her?"

"I arrested her once already."

He tips his head side to side. "Yeah, but a warrant is very different than being a suspect in an active case. Things with you and Kamea…"

"They're great," I half-lie.

Although they're good, ever since that night at the bar, Kamea feels withdrawn. She hasn't said anything to make me think she's still bothered about what happened. And she's always got a smile. We still have sex and she's right there with me every time. She came in just this morning and slid into bed with me after her shift at Rian's. There's nothing that says something is wrong, but I feel as if maybe she's still holding back.

"Good. Well, I just wanted to warn you." He shuffles through his papers as though he's ready for me to leave now.

"Captain, any word on the detective position?"

He smiles. "I heard announcements will be made tomorrow morning. I haven't heard any specifics yet. I'll let you know if I do hear something. Otherwise, tomorrow."

I nod. "Thanks."

"You're welcome." I walk out, and when my hand lands on the door, Cap calls, "Whelan?"

I glance over my shoulder.

"I'm really proud of you. You grew up overnight."

"Excuse me?"

"The relationship you had with Leilani must have been all about the bedroom because you didn't fit with her. I get it, I forced it with my second wife. I was so hell-bent on being married again after my first wife screwed me over that I forced a relationship that never should've happened. We all do it. Don't beat yourself up about it, but don't let Kamea slip out of your grasp with any 'what-if' scenarios."

"Yes, sir," I say and walk out, his words not registering until I'm out of the office.

Patrice walks by me with her special tea the fertility doctor gave her to induce ovulation. "Ready, cowboy?"

I follow her out to the car, dissecting the captain's words. Did I force things with Leilani just because I had been screwed over by my college girlfriend?

No. I shake my head. Those feelings for her were real. They're gone now, but they were real at the time. They had to be.

"Hey, I'm going to drive if you don't get out of this comatose state you're in." Patrice dangles the keys in front of my face.

I'm so sick of thinking about Leilani, I snatch them out of her hand and climb into the driver's seat. Leilani's been way too much a part of my life than she ever should've been.

Once we're on the road, Patrice babbles about her procedures and how she might have to go on desk duty.

I smile and act interested, but as soon as she stops for breath, I interrupt. "I'm desperate to get Kamea to understand that she's the one for me. That Leilani means nothing compared to how I feel about her. How can I do that?"

Patrice laughs and glances over. "About damn time. How about you take the girl out on a damn date? Without your friends."

"We do go on dates."

"Looking for Leilani is not a date. Going to a bar with your friends is not a date. You making her an omelet in the morning is not a date. And fucking like bunnies is not a date."

My lips press into a straight line. "I tell you too much shit."

She giggles. "I'm masterful in getting information out of you. But you need to show her, not just tell her."

When Patrice puts it that way, all those damn insecurities

from when I was younger and people assumed I was dumb resurface. Should I have known this?

"Woo her and make her swoon," Patrice says. "Flowers. Dinners. Cards. Poetry."

Poetry? She can't be serious. I can't write a poem. I don't know what Kamea's favorite flower is or whether she has a favorite vegetarian restaurant. Then it occurs to me that I probably should know those things. Damn, maybe I am messing up this boyfriend thing.

I pull the car into the parking lot of a drugstore.

"What are you doing?" Patrice asks.

"I'm getting a card."

She blows out a breath and laughs. "You don't waste any time."

I put the car in park. "I might not know how to make a woman swoon, but I'm going to woo her so hard she'll want to be Mrs. Knox Whelan."

Patrice rolls her eyes and grabs the handle of the door.

"Nope, I can pick this one out on my own," I say and exit the car.

How could I have been so stupid? I'll show her exactly how much I think she's the one for me. Watch out, Kamea. Your Prince Charming was a little late to the party, but he's on his way now.

I CALL Kamea after my shift—since I know she'll be up— and confirm that she's still planning to come down to the courthouse. As the arresting officer I have to be present in case I'm asked to speak. I'm hoping the fact that we might run into Leilani won't stir up bad feelings for her, but we have to find out if Leilani shows up at court because Kamea should get her money back. Not to move out or change anything happening in our lives, but because she deserves it.

I wait on the steps of the courthouse with the card I got for Kamea stuffed in the inside of my leather jacket. I'm still worried about the detective job being announced today. It would be great to be able to celebrate that with her.

I catch Kamea walking up the street in her jeans, boots, and heavy jacket. She's got on a rainbow-colored hat and gloves that match. I smile as she retrieves some change from her pocket and puts it in a Salvation Army red bucket, and the Santa jingles his bell at her in thanks. That puts a smile on her face. I swear when she's smiling, I've never seen someone more beautiful.

The short wait for Kamea to cross the street to meet me feels like forever. Her eyes catch mine when she's midway into the pedestrian walkway, and that smile she gave Santa isn't anything compared to her smile right now. It's infectious, and I'm fairly sure I look like a goon smiling back at her.

"Hey, you," she says, bouncing the last few steps before rising up on her tiptoes to kiss me. "Thanks for reminding me. Though I told you I don't really care about the money anymore."

I wrap my arm around her waist and pull her toward me, locking her to my chest. "I missed you last night."

"I missed you too."

"I have a surprise for you, but after." I slide my hand in hers.

"Oh, a surprise." She doesn't beg me for more information which I thought for sure she would. "Can't wait."

Doesn't every woman love a surprise so much she can barely contain herself until she finds out what it is?

"You don't want to pry it out of me?" I open the door to the courthouse and we stand in the security line.

"Nope."

"Why not?"

She takes off her hat and stuffs it, along with her gloves, inside her jacket. After pulling her purse over her head, she lays it on the conveyor belt and steps through the metal detector, going through without a problem. I show my badge and gun and they pull me aside. I'm wanded while Kamea gets herself organized. After we're done, I entwine our hands again, and I lead her to the courtroom Leilani should be appearing in. We sit in the back, and I place my hand on her knee. She rests her head on my shoulder for a moment as though she's tired.

"Why don't you want to know the surprise?" I ask again.

She giggles. "Because I like surprises. I'm eager to find out, but if I dig it out of you, it's not a surprise anymore."

I place my finger under her chin and lift it toward me, kissing her on the lips.

"Come on. This is a courthouse. Don't push me to arrest you for public indecency." Patrice sits down next to us.

"Hey, Patrice," Kamea says.

"Why are you here?" I ask.

Kamea smacks my stomach.

"I'm invested in this whole thing too," Patrice says. "I had to see if she showed."

Patrice doesn't have to be here since I signed off on the paperwork. She's choosing to.

We all sit there and listen to case after case until they announce Leilani's. I grab Kamea's hand and squeeze it, wondering if Leilani's out in the hall. Maybe she lawyered up and the lawyer will speak on her behalf. But the judge checks the clock and looks at the bailiff. I've seen that look before.

"Next case," the judge says.

The bailiff takes the paperwork from the judge and

carries it over to the record keeper. Leilani now has a warrant out for her arrest.

My phone vibrates in my pocket, and I slide it out to see that it's the station.

"I'll meet you in the hall," I whisper and excuse myself down the row and out the doors. I look around, hoping I see Leilani. Not showing up to court has taken her misbehavior to a new level.

I answer my phone. "Hello?"

"Officer Whelan?"

My stomach tightens with anticipation. "Yes, this is he."

"This is Chief Jenkins. I just wanted to be the first to congratulate you on the detective position. We're happy to have someone like you on board in our investigative department. You did excellent on your detective's exam, and your interview filled in the picture of what kind of cop you are. Captain Donnelly has all the information for you, but I needed to offer my congratulations."

I feel almost as if I'm floating. In a way, his words sound surreal. "Thank you so much."

"You're very welcome. I'll see you at the swearing-in ceremony. Have a great day, Officer Whelan."

"You too, sir. Thank you." I click off the phone and stuff it in my pocket.

Patrice and Kamea walk out of the courtroom, and I run over and pick up Kamea.

"I got it," I say, swinging her in a circle.

"I knew you would." Her arms tighten around my neck. "Congratulations! We need to celebrate."

I lower her to the floor. "Not yet. First, I'm taking you out. A real date where I can woo you."

"Woo me?" She giggles.

Patrice gives me a thumbs-up from behind Kamea's back and waves goodbye.

"Yes, I'm wooing you."

"Well, you don't have to, but I'm super excited to see what's involved." She raises on her tiptoes, stopping when her lips are millimeters from mine. "Congratulations, Detective Whelan," she says before kissing me.

I pull her into me until someone clears their throat as they walk by. "Let's get out of here."

I take her hand, and although Kamea didn't get her money, I feel as if there's closure now that Leilani's court date is over. Whatever happens, happens. All I care about is Kamea and the two of us moving forward together.

CHAPTER TWENTY-NINE

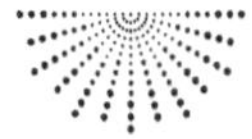

Kamea

I borrow a blouse of Rian's and pair it with my dark slim-fit jeans in the hopes it's fancy enough for wherever Knox has planned. He's not exactly a five-star restaurant guy, which is something I love about him. I don't even need this date for him to woo me, although I appreciate the effort.

A card slides under my bedroom door at Rian and Dylan's. I can't stay here forever. I know that. From Dylan's reactions and body language when we're alone together, I'm not really welcome. But like all his friends, Dylan does what the woman in his life wants rather than what he wants.

I pick up the card to find my name written in guy's handwriting. When I slide my finger under the seam, my stomach feels fizzy with nerves and excitement. It dawns on me that Knox and I have a lot to find out about one another still. I have no idea when his birthday even is.

I take the card out of the envelope, sitting on the edge of my bed, and read "I'm bananas for you" on the outside. Inside, there's a short note.

Kamea,

I've never been so happy, and it's because of you coming into my life. I'm so thankful we found our way to one another again. Rest assured, you're on my mind every minute of every day. Although I'd like you to move back home, at least you're only across the hall, but please come back home. :)

Pick you up in a half hour.

Love,
Knox

I giggle and stuff the card in the top drawer of the dresser, under my panties and bras. I'm ready early, so I examine myself in the full-length mirror that must have been Sierra's. My makeup is on, my hair is done. We're not one of these couples who have to resort to this stupid dating where he picks me up and I act as if I'm still putting on lipstick when he arrives.

Taking the small clutch Rian loaned me, I walk out the bedroom door. Dylan is sprawled out on the couch, remote in hand. Rian walks over with a bowl of popcorn, and Dylan slides to make room for her.

That's what I want. That's relationship goals for me. The comfortableness of lying around and watching a movie or Netflix. Not some uptight restaurant where I imagine eyes are on me.

"Where are you going?" Rian asks.

"I'm going over there. It's stupid for me to wait here."

"But… did you get the card?" Rian asks, biting her lip.

I raise my eyebrows in question. "I did. Thanks for delivering it."

"So stay and wait for him to get you."

I wave her off. "Nah, I mean, we were living together for a while. Plus, I'm eager to see him."

Rian looks at Dylan. "Remember when we couldn't wait a half hour to see one another?"

He kisses her cheek. "I still can't wait a half hour to see you."

Rian giggles and bends down to kiss him.

"That's my sign. Have a great night." I leave their apartment and step out into the hallway at the same time Jax is walking down the hall from the elevator.

"Hey, look at you." His gaze roams over me, but not in a creepy way and definitely not a sexual way. "Hot date?"

"With your roommate."

He inserts his key into their apartment door lock. "Lucky him."

I shove him lightly. "Your T-shirts are moving again. The post office lost them but I looked and they're finally being tracked so they should be here soon."

Now I want to be there when he reveals them just to see Frankie's reaction. She's sure to be annoyed. I don't know her well, but what I do know makes me think she won't tolerate his adolescent pranks.

We open the door. I hear the shower on and see a bouquet of flowers and a box of chocolates on the table.

"Damn, I'm crashing at Dylan's tonight. You guys can have the place." Jax opens the fridge and grabs a beer. "Want anything to drink while you're waiting?"

I shake my head. "I'm good. I think I'm going to go wait in his bedroom and surprise him." I grin.

Jax groans. "Shit, I'm packing shit and getting the hell out of here before you two go at it before the actual date." He guzzles his beer on the way to his room.

The shower turns off, so I only have a minute before Knox gets out wearing only a towel. I slip off my shoes so they don't make any noise on the hardwood. I tiptoe across the room, my heels hanging from my fingers.

I turn the knob of his bedroom door and it creaks a bit as it always does. The room is dark since in winter, Cliffton Heights is dark by five o'clock most days. I slide in and shut the door.

The lamp on the nightstand turns on, and the surprise of the blinding light—as well as knowing it's not Knox since he's in the shower—startles me. But the thin figure in the sheets causes me to step back.

"Oh, Kamea, I'm so sorry. Knox wanted to shower before he told you." Leilani cringes.

I blink a few times to make sure it really is Leilani lying naked in Knox's bed. "I'm sorry?"

She sits up and the blanket falls, revealing a hickey on her right breast. "I came here to talk to him because of the whole court thing, and it just kind of happened. Guess the flame between us just can't be extinguished."

She looks sincere. Like she did after the night she dragged me out of the party. Like she truly wants what's good for me.

"Are you suggesting that you and he…"

She bites her lip and nods, glancing down at herself as though she didn't realize the sheet fell. "Whoops, you probably know how crazy he gets in bed. Always throwing me around like he wants to crawl inside me."

I cough and gag as bile rises up my throat. He's never like that with me. He holds me with gentle hands, praises my body and how much he loves it. He's never screwed me in wild abandonment.

"It's so not like us to have sex in a bed. You know?"

She's still talking while I'm fairly sure my jaw is hanging open as I process everything, my mind running a million miles a minute. We were on our way to something so great. Surely, he wouldn't write me that card then do this.

Then again, Leilani has always had a hold on him. Something I couldn't compete with.

"I really am sorry. I know how much it takes for you to get close to someone. But you know Jax is a great guy. Maybe you two could, you know?"

"Kamea?" Knox says from behind me. I didn't even hear him come in. He's wearing just a towel, his chest still glistening with a few drops of water.

I stare at him, waiting for his reaction.

His vision follows mine to the bed. "Leilani?"

"Why is she in your bed?" I try really hard to keep my voice even and not burst into tears.

Knox shakes his head. What, did he have some kind of out-of-body experience so he doesn't remember sucking on her right breast so hard he marred her? "What the hell are you doing here?"

Leilani giggles. "It's okay, babe, I told her. This way you don't have to be the bad guy."

I throw my heels at Knox. "Say something!"

He snaps out of whatever state he was in. "There isn't anything to say. I have no idea why she's here!"

"So she's lying? How did she get in here when you were in the shower then?" I ask, adrenaline racing through my body causing my heart to beat like a bass drum.

"I have no idea."

"Stop bullshitting her, Knox. Just tell her the truth. She'll handle it better than you think." Leilani climbs out of bed, taking Knox's T-shirt from the edge of the mattress and sliding it onto her body. She steps over to him and rises up on her tiptoes.

When Knox sees her intention, he darts away before she can kiss him. "You haven't answered how you got in here."

Leilani pouts. "I still have a key to the apartment."

He pushes her away. "Which I need back now."

"She has a key? You never changed your locks?" I yell.

"What the hell is going on?" Jax comes in, beer in hand. His eyes zero in on Leilani. "What the hell?"

"Hey, Jax," she says.

"Oh fuck," he says and runs his hand through his hair.

Pure rage soars through my veins with the speed of lightning and I cock my fist back and punch Leilani right in the face.

"*Holy shit!*" Jax yells, full-out laughing.

"Fuck. Help me," Knox tells him.

Leilani grabs my hair before I can move back.

"Do you like inserting yourself into my life?" she whispers so only I hear her. "Just slide right in and take my man?"

"He's not yours."

I unwind her fingers from my hair and wrestle her to the bed, straddling her.

"Stop!" Knox yells.

"I'm going to get the Jell-O," Jax says.

"Stop joking around. I have no fucking clue what's going on." Knox hooks his arms under my armpits and pries me, kicking and screaming, off Leilani. "She's not worth this," he says softly.

But he gets my feet to the floor. Leilani sits up in the bed, Knox's T-shirt sagging down her body. I can't stand seeing her wearing his clothes.

"I can't do this." I turn to leave.

"Admit it." She follows me. "You've always been jealous of me. It's like some Single White Female shit you got going on with me. You want my life."

I whip around. "Your life? You don't have a life. You

trapeze your way from person to person, never making an honest connection with anyone. I was jealous of you once upon a time. The braveness you showed when you left home and the fact that nothing seems to scare you. But…" I step forward. "If something doesn't scare you, then you've never truly loved something."

She huffs. "So you love Knox? Is that what you're suggesting? What have you guys been dating for? Like, a week?"

My gaze falls to Knox, and he looks as if he's waiting for me to answer the question. He should be telling her. He's the common denominator between us. Why isn't he telling her how much he loves me? That he doesn't care about her anymore? He just stands there silently, waiting for me to pour out all my feelings. No fucking way will I give him that satisfaction.

I weave around her and grab my shoes, then put them on one at a time. "You know what? Have one another. I might've gotten caught up in all this, but I'm washing my hands of it all. I hope you're happy together." I grab my clutch and storm out of the apartment.

"Hold up." Jax follows me into the hallway. "Where are you going?"

"I need to get the hell out of here."

He nods as if he understands completely. I walk to the elevator and press the down button. It arrives in record time. I step in and press one for the main level.

"*Wait! Kamea!*" Knox yells, then he's between the closing crack of the two metal doors. "Stop."

But I'm not even sure he means it. I let the doors shut in his face and ride down to the main floor. I walk by the over-filled recycling bin with all the flyers and junk mail. I'm a sucker for punishment, so I decide to head to the one place that will remind me that my decision just now was the right one.

CHAPTER THIRTY

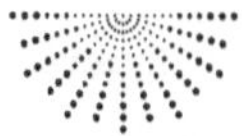

Knox

I shove Jax in the chest, walking back down the hallway to our apartment. "How could you let her leave?"

"Because her staying here with you acting like a mute motherfucker isn't gonna help."

The door across the hall opens and Dylan pops out, shirt-less and his hair everywhere.

"Did we interrupt your fucking session?" Jax asks.

"What the hell is going on?" he asks.

Our apartment door swings open to reveal Leilani in my shirt. Fuck.

"Get the hell out of my shirt," I yell, causing another door to open up down the hall.

"Surprise! Leilani's back!" Jax injects faux happiness into his tone.

"Where's Kamea?" Rian says behind Dylan, clearly upset.

"Oh my God, she did a real number on all of you. She's not as sweet as she seems," Leilani says.

"Sweeter than you," Rian says, disappearing inside and coming out a second later with her purse and her coat in hand.

Blanca walks out of their apartment down the hall. "What's going on?"

Rian puts one arm in her jacket. "Kamea needs us."

"Babe, give me a second I'll go with you." Dylan disappears inside.

Another apartment door opens up and Evan and Seth join the party.

"What the heck?" Evan says, pointing at Leilani.

Seth puts his arm around Evan's shoulders. "Seriously. When will she learn to stay away?"

"Nice, Seth," Leilani sneers.

"Just go the fuck inside and get dressed in your own clothes. Take my damn T-shirt off." Surprisingly, she does it.

I shut my apartment door and face my friends.

"Why are you only wearing a towel, Knox?" Evan asks.

"Babe, are you checking him out?" Seth ask and Evan rolls her eyes.

"Never mind that. You guys go look for Kamea. I'm going to stay back and talk to her."

The groans from each of my friends says what they think of that idea.

I put up my hands. "I love Kamea. And I'm going after her, but this is unfinished business that has to be dealt with before Kamea and I can move forward. I can't risk Leilani popping up any time she feels like fucking with my life. Please, go look for Kamea. I have no idea where she would've gone. If you find her, text me and I'll meet you there. This shouldn't take that long. I'm just making sure she understands that it's over once and for all."

Seth puts his hand on my shoulder. "She's got the powers of Maleficent. Are you sure someone shouldn't stay behind and make sure you actually end it?"

I smack his hand off my shoulder. "Yes, asshole. She no longer has any power over me. I know I fucked up many times, but Kamea is the one for me. Leilani is just a speed-bump before I can get to Kamea."

All my friends nod.

Dylan comes out of their apartment. "Let's go. And I just want to warn you, I was a minute away from getting laid, so you owe me big for this. Get your love life together, man."

"Dylan." Rian puts her hand on his arm. "Let's remember—"

"When your head was messing up your decisions!" Jax says.

Dylan thinks about what Jax said and nods as if conceding Jax's point.

"Just keep me informed." I want to go after Kamea so bad, but I need to make sure Leilani goes far, far away.

I walk into my apartment and shut the door, flipping the lock in case any of my friends think I'm an idiot and would ruin my chances with Kamea. Leilani's getting dressed with my door open, so I grab a water out of the fridge. It's only then I realize I'm still in just a towel. Fuck.

She comes out of my room. "Happy?" She holds her hands out to her side, her bra hanging off her finger. "I left my bra off just in case. We can skip a step."

She just doesn't quit, does she?

I growl deep in my throat. But then again, hasn't this always been the way it was with us? She'd seduce me, and since I thought she was the one for me, I'd let her. What a complete jackass I was.

"I'll be back." I go to my bedroom and hurriedly dress in my jeans and Henley because it would be just like her to walk in on me. On purpose. I'm surprised she doesn't actually.

I peek into the living room and see that she's made herself comfortable, drinking a beer on the couch with a bag of chips in her lap while she watches television. I shake my head then grab my phone off the nightstand and text Patrice.

I step into the living room and sit in the chair across from her. "You are aware there's a warrant out for your arrest, right?"

"Yeah, I was thinking you could fix that for me."

"Why would I?"

She giggles. "Because you're my Knox."

"Meaning?" I arch an eyebrow.

"Can we please stop this? I get that you had your fun with my lookalike, but I'm back. I know I was horrible, and I should've never run away. It took me a long time to realize what was good for me, but I want you back, baby. I want a future with you." She puts the chips and beer on the table and pushes herself up off the couch.

She's got to be fucking kidding me.

I hold up my hand before she gets too far. "Stay there."

She nibbles on her cheek and wiggles her body before sitting down. "Want to play?" She grabs the hem of her shirt and inches it up. "I'm up for playing the little bad girl. You can punish me."

"Fuck, Leilani." I stand from the chair and it bounces backward, falling to the floor from the force of my ejection. "What don't you get? I'm not attracted to you anymore."

She blows out a breath. "Oh, but you are to Kamea? We're practically the same person."

"You're wrong there." I sit on a breakfast stool, feeling safer. "She's nothing like you."

"I'm cooler."

"What are you, twelve?" I scowl.

"I'm just saying. She's always wanted to be me. Always following me and copying what I did. Of course she wanted you—because she knows how much I love you. Can't you see, it's all just a setup? C'mon Knox, you can't be dumb enough to really fall for her." She grabs a chip and puts it in her mouth.

I hate that her accusation of being dumb pisses me off. "You never wanted me. If you did, you wouldn't have left me so many times."

She stands. "Not true. It just wasn't our time. Our time is now. I want to settle down with you."

I remain silent for a moment, Kamea running through my brain. I'm fucking this up the longer I'm in here with Leilani. *Just put the dirt over the coffin, Knox.* Nothing is gonna come from dragging this out.

"I love her," I say with conviction I hope Leilani hears. I inwardly wince that Kamea isn't the first to hear me say it. "She's everything I've always wanted. She's everything you're not."

Her smile finally drops, and she looks as if I smacked her across the face. "What does that mean? Does she let you fuck her anywhere you want? Does she play your little role-playing games?"

"I don't want any of that with her because I don't need to pretend she's anyone other than who she is."

Leilani guffaws. "You can't be serious. Did you read that somewhere?"

"She's caring and sweet and listens to me. We have a mutual respect. It's not all me doing things for her. She does things for me too."

"Well, you gave her a place to stay. Of course she does."

I tilt my head. "How did you know that?"

She blows out a breath. "I have my ways. I was glad you

let her live with you, but falling in love with her? Come on. Get real."

"Remember that night I first met you?"

"How could I forget? Sex in the alley? That was hot."

"I was hitting on Kamea first that night. But I didn't want to be hurt again, and my buddy said she was the kind of girl you take home to Mom. Then you breezed in and you definitely weren't that type, so we hooked up."

Her eyes narrow. I didn't mean to hurt her. Okay, I do want to hurt her a little because of the hurtful things she said to Kamea and the way she played with my feelings for so long. But mostly I want to stress that Kamea is the one for me and she's not some fill-in for Leilani.

"Are you trying to hurt me because I left you?" she asks.

I shake my head. "I want you to understand. I actually saw her first."

She looks away and inhales deeply. "I can't believe this. I help her not get date-raped in high school, I leave my family because of the bullies, and this is how she repays me— stealing my boyfriend?"

"I wasn't your boyfriend to steal," I say.

"You're more mine than hers."

I stifle a laugh. "Not true."

She throws her arms in the air. "So you have no feelings for me anymore?"

I shake my head, one hundred percent confident in my truth.

"That's it?"

A knock sounds on the door, and I step back to open it. "No." I open the door and Patrice and her new partner Hank stand in the doorway, dressed in uniform. "You have an outstanding warrant for your arrest."

"Hey, Leilani, remember me? Patrice." My partner points

at herself. "I know it's been a while. We can do this the easy way or the hard way."

Patrice turns Leilani around, and Leilani doesn't fight the cuffs as I thought she might.

"I cannot believe you're doing this," Leilani seethes.

"Yeah, you look nothing like Kamea." Patrice winks at me and escorts Leilani out of my apartment.

"You cannot be serious? Knox? Fine, we're over, but you don't have to turn me in. *Knox!*" she screams as they take her down the hall.

I put on my shoes, grab my jacket and my keys, and run down the stairs instead of joining them in the elevator. In my texts, I go to the group chat with everyone in it.

Me: *Anyone find her?*

Seth: *Not yet. We've checked Riverfront.*

Blanca: *She's not at any of the restaurants downtown.*

Jax: *She's not at the liquor stores.*

Evan: *Why would she be at a liquor store?*

Jax: *That's where I would be.*

Rian: *We've checked Sweet Infusion and the Cliffton Heights Country Club. Dylan has a place in mind. We'll let you know.*

Me: *I'm checking with her old building manager in Peekskil. You find her, call me ASAP.*

Seth: *Dare I ask about Leilani?*

I blow out a breath, sitting in my Bronco and watching the cop car pull away.

Me: *It's done.*

I feel as though Kamea should be the first to know that Patrice arrested her.

Five minutes later, right before I get on the highway, a text comes in.

Rian: *We found her. 56 N. Wells St.*

That address sounds so familiar, but I can't place it. I put it in my GPS and follow directions to the opposite side of Cliffton Heights. Turns out it's somewhere I haven't been in a long damn time.

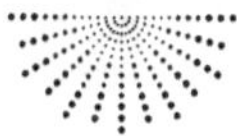

CHAPTER THIRTY-ONE

Kamea

Years ago, it was a dive bar for college kids and anyone in their early twenties. Now, it's a pretend spy bar. The entrance is hidden, and if you don't know the password to get in, they make you do something wacky to gain entry. Lucky for me, a couple was walking out and I think the woman could tell something was off with me, so she whispered to me, "Sterling Archer," and the guy with her pointed me in the right direction.

Entering the dark room, I pay my cover charge and give the password to the bouncer, who seems surprised I know it. Maybe he sees my red-rimmed eyes and the pity train of my life continues. He allows me in, and I find a spot in a round booth on the back wall, away from anyone.

Everyone else in the bar seems like regulars or are thrilled to be at a spy bar where you have to answer riddles and complete missions. I'm not quite sure why I even came here. Okay, that's a lie. He broke me here.

I'll have to face Knox eventually. With some distance, I feel almost positive that he doesn't want Leilani anymore, but I couldn't stand seeing the two of them together in the same room. It felt like a knife going through my heart.

The three of us have come to the point where he can really truly choose between us once again. I guess on some level, I always knew it would come to this, and that's what always set me on edge whenever Leilani was mentioned. Though I think when I return to the apartment it will be me he chooses, I have to prepare myself that it might not be.

I'm half done with my Agent Spytini drink when a man slides into the booth across from me. I look up from sucking as much alcohol through my straw as possible and see that it's Dylan. "How did you find me?"

"Well, I sure as fuck didn't know you'd go to a place like this, but this was Duke's once upon a time, no?"

I nod.

"Rian had this idea you might have gone to Duke's because that's where you and Knox first met."

I nod again. Smart woman.

"You didn't catch us on the camera?" He points toward the TVs at the bar. I kind of remember people laughing every few minutes. "If you don't know the password, you have to do stupid shit like the chicken dance to get in. They show it for everyone in here to see."

I shrug. "Where is Rian?" I look around the room. She has a better chance than Dylan of cheering me up. The man hates me.

"She's at the bar, trying to figure out a riddle. I asked her to give me five minutes alone with you."

I sip my drink, and it slurps, saying my time with Agent

Spytini is over. Dylan flags down the waitress and orders another for me and a beer for him.

"Why would you want to do that?" I push away the empty glass. "You don't like me."

His head sways right and left as though I have a point. "It's not that I don't like you. I'm cautious of you."

I nod. "Okay."

The waitress comes back and I'm thankful to have the distraction of another drink.

Dylan sips his beer and holds it over the table. "I've been friends with Knox for a long time. He's a good guy."

"I know."

He nods. "Leilani hurt him."

My forehead falls to the table. If I hear this one more time, I'm going to scream.

"I guess I should say I've seen him go after these women who don't have any hopes and dreams or aspirations for the future. He had this girl in college who was the worst. It was a blessing they broke up, otherwise, she would have sucked him dry. I'm fairly sure she went to college to find a husband. But she fucked it up by cheating on him. A few nights later, we were here." He looks around. "Much different then though."

I nod.

"That night, Jimmy told him not to go for you because you were the take-home-to-mom type of girl. Jimmy's a jackass, by the way. And so, Knox took Leilani home. In the end, she fucked with his head." I groan, and he holds up his hand. "I'm not going to talk about her, but when you re-entered his life, I saw it for the first time."

"What?" I groan.

"A woman who deserved him."

"You sound like you're his mother or something."

He chuckles and sips his beer. "He's done me solids our

entire friendship, and I wish that night when we were here, I would've told him Jimmy was wrong and he should've taken you home."

Another round of applause and cheers ring out when more people come into the bar.

"Well, he didn't choose me."

"Yeah, he didn't. All I can tell you is he regrets it. I see it. He was never a guy who could just have sex and not have commitment. Not sure why he thought he could. That's reserved for us foster kid fuck-ups who turn off their feelings."

I glance at Rian. "I doubt that."

"Jax," Dylan says as an example. "I've graduated. Thank God for Rian. But she had to do a lot of shit to get me where I am now. I never thought I was good enough for her. That's the problem with growing up like we did."

"I want to make his life better. I know I let him house me and I shouldn't have but—"

He lifts his hand. "Rian says it's none of my business and she's right. It's not. You would think, from where I come from, that I would understand the exchange between you two. I do it at my shop all the time. I give newbies a place to hone their skills. Knox would've taken you in whether or not he was attracted to you, but I think the fact that he was probably helped. I guess I thought you were going to use him. And then when you played that game and moved into our apartment—"

"But I did it because—"

Again, he holds up his hand. "I get it now. But I'm just going to tell you this. I know you're upset because… of her."

I smile that he didn't say her name.

"But when he's with you, it's completely different. He's happier and laid-back. He's himself. She had this way of keeping him on edge. You get along with his parents and all of us."

"Some of you," I say.

He smiles. "I'm protective. He's my boy."

I nod, happy that someone looks out for Knox since he thinks it's his job to look after everyone else.

"Give him a second chance." Dylan turns his head toward the camera all the other patrons are staring at.

Knox is on the screen, showing his badge and arguing with the bouncer. But the bouncer is having none of it. The crowd goes wild with screams and chants of "Make the cop beg!"

Dylan's hand covers mine. "Believe me, I don't vouch for a lot of guys, but that one… he'll keep your heart safe. And if he doesn't, you can kick me in the balls." He takes his beer and walks away.

The bouncer makes Knox pretend he's making out with himself, wrapping his arms around his chest and running them over his back. After he's done, the patrons cheer and the bouncer lets him through. The door opens and they all clap and cheer. But Knox ignores them, searching the room. I watch from my dark corner of the bar. He finds Dylan first and he in turn points at me. I dodge eye contact with Knox as if my drink is the most interesting thing in the world.

But a second later, Knox slides into the booth with me. Unlike the last one, this man doesn't stay on the other side. He slides all the way in beside me until he can grab my hands.

"Don't end this," Knox says. "I have no idea why she thought I'd want her back. I would never do that to you. I don't want her. I want you. Only you. You have to believe me. What do I have to do to prove it?" I say nothing, and he continues. "I know Dylan beat me here, but I had to make sure she knows there's no shot. That you're the one who owns me."

"Own? Should I get a leash?"

He smiles and the waitress comes over, but he puts up a hand. "If you want. But… hold up."

He stops and slides out of the booth, walking away.

What is he doing? My gaze follows Knox, but he gets swallowed by the crowd. Two minutes later, the waitress comes over with a drink and slides it my way.

"Oh no, this is enough. Otherwise, I'll be on your floor by closing time."

She laughs. "No, this is from the gentleman at the bar." She points.

Knox tips his beer bottle my way as Rian and Dylan pretend they don't know what he's doing.

"Tell him thanks."

"This is a cute little game you two play," she says and walks away.

Then Knox stands from the bar with his beer in his hand and walks through the throng of people, his eyes on me the entire time. Stopping at the edge of the booth, he signals at the empty spot. "Can I sit down?"

"Sure," I say.

He sits, ignoring my questioning expression. "I'm Knox."

I can't help but smile. "Kamea."

"Knox and Kamea sound pretty good together," he says, and I giggle.

"Would that have been your line?"

He chuckles. "I'm sorry, have we met before?"

I roll my eyes.

"I would've asked you to dance." He looks around. "But I'm guessing I have to ask you to complete a mission with me?"

"I don't even know you," I play along.

"What do you want to know?" he asks.

"Whatever you want to tell me about yourself." I sip my drink.

"I fell in love with you on the way over here."

"All the way from the bar?"

He chuckles. "Something like that." He winks and slides out of the booth and holds out his hand. "What do you say? Trust me?"

This is it. This is the moment I either decide to leave the past and my insecurities aside and charge forward into my life with this man and see what comes of it, or I let my fear and doubts steal something that could be pretty great.

I slide my hand into his with a cleansing breath. "I trust you."

And I do. Because somewhere along the way, I fell in love with him too.

Everyone points at the television—it's all our other friends, trying to gain entry. Jax refuses to do the Macarena with everyone else though.

"Leave it to Jax."

Knox wraps his arms around my waist, using one hand to tuck my hair behind my ear. "I mean it. I love you. So much. And I should've picked you all those years ago."

I poke him in the chest. "You should have."

"I'm a lucky man to have a chance at a do-over."

I laugh and shake my head. "Yeah, you are."

"You don't have to say it back or anything, you know. Just in case you think I'm waiting or something."

"Okay."

"I mean, I don't want to pressure you. When you're ready, that's when you should say it."

I pretend to slide into the booth, but right before I get in, I turn around. "Hey, Knox?"

"Yeah?"

"I love you."

He laughs, his hands landing on my hips and swinging me around. "I knew it." And as he lowers me back down, he holds me tight. "I promise you, we'll have a story for the books."

"I think we already do."

His lips press to mine, sealing our fate with a kiss that makes my knees weak. Good things really are worth waiting for.

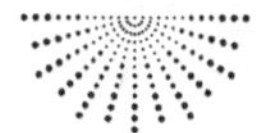

Knox

It's our first official date, although I'm picking her up at the bedroom we share. But it's about time I show her what a future with Knox Whelan is really about.

I knock on our bedroom door and she opens it, wearing a skirt and tights and a short sweater that fits snuggly over her tits.

"On second thought, a night in sounds nice," I say, stepping into the room.

She puts her hand on my chest and shakes her head. "Nope. We're going on the date. The bed will be here when we return."

"You should've dressed down."

She quirks an eyebrow. "Um… the whole point of a date is so you have to imagine having sex with me the entire night."

"Then we can skip the date because that's me every day.

Trust me when I say that if I'm not actually fucking you, I'm thinking about fucking you."

She slides past me. "Aren't you the romantic."

I snatch her up with my arm around her waist and pull her back into me. "Look at the table."

She turns her head to find a big box on the table. It doesn't hold flowers and candies like I bought for the night when she-who-shall-remain-nameless ruined it all.

I kiss her on the neck. "Go open it."

She walks over to our kitchen table and opens the box, looks back at me for a moment, then closes the box back up. "Nope."

"Yes."

"Nope." She grabs her purse. "Let's go on our date before we end up in a fight."

"Holy shit!" Jax comes out of his room, holding a big box and sporting a black T-shirt with the lettering "Jax Inked Me and I Loved It."

I turn toward Kamea, who raises both eyebrows and her shoulders.

"Frankie is going to kick your ass," I say to Jax.

He laughs. "I know."

"Hold up," I say.

He stops before exiting the apartment.

Yes, Jax lives with us because this is us. We seem to all jive together, and it enabled me to set up the third room for Kamea's T-shirt business. That's my big surprise for later tonight, but if she can't accept a box full of T-shirts, she might not accept a room with a press and printer either.

I point at Kamea. "Tell her to accept my gift. That I'm wooing her."

Jax sets down the box and puts his hand on her shoulder. "He's wooing you. Not trying to own you."

"I've never thought own," she says. "Saving is more what I was thinking."

"I'm not trying to save you. I'm your boyfriend and I'm helping you. Think of it as an early Christmas gift." I wrap my arms around her waist and pull her toward me. "You have to let me do nice things for you."

"Not buy products for my company." Her forehead hits my chest.

"I'm out. Gonna show Seth first." Jax continues out the door with the box, laughing as he leaves.

"Please? I really wanted to do something nice for you."

"Flowers and candy…"

"Aren't us. I'm not going to write you poetry or bring home flowers every night. That's not us. You cook for me when you're wooing me, and I buy you stuff to make your life easier to woo you."

Her head moves back and forth. "Ugh… Knox…" She looks up. "I'm paying for dinner tonight then."

"No," I say.

She opens the door and heads out into the hall. "We're not having this argument. I'm paying if you want me to accept that present."

I think I'll wait until after we have sex to show her the room I transformed for her. "I pay."

She presses the button on the elevator, humming.

Seth's apartment door opens down the hall, and he and Evan come out with Jax as Seth says, "I'm gonna record this because it's gonna go viral."

Everyone gets on the elevator, including Jax and his big-ass plastic container of shirts. When we get to the first floor, I find my mom waiting at the elevator.

"Mom?" I ask.

"Hey, Mama Whelan. I got something for you." Jax kisses

her cheek, sets down the plastic container, and hands her one of the T-shirts.

She reads it and beams. "I'll be proud to wear this."

"Um. No." I snatch it and toss it back into the container.

"That's not nice. I'm proud to wear something Kamea designed that advertises Jax." She grabs it again before Jax shuts the container. "You look very beautiful," she says to Kamea.

"Thank you, Peggy. Knox is taking me on a date." Kamea slides her arm through mine.

Although Kamea talks to her brother, her parents haven't come around. My mom says we should just book plane tickets and go down, but I'm not sure that's what's best for Kamea. To my mom, family is everything, so I don't think she understands how Kamea's parents have gone so long without being in contact with her.

"Why are you here?" I ask my mom.

"I have a letter. Jolie's." She digs in her purse and holds it up. "I'm sure Frankie would want to know what Jolie asked Santa for, and I forgot to pass it on at the shelter that night. When you were younger, you'd change your mind the day before Christmas and I'd end up chasing the item down anyway so you'd believe in Santa." She looks at Kamea. "Glad those days are over."

"Come with me. I'm showing off my shirts to Frankie. You can give her the letter then," Jax says.

"Oh, that's nice."

"Yeah, Frankie's going to kick him in the balls," Seth adds, his phone poised and ready.

"Well, let's go see the show before we head out," Kamea says.

I shrug. "Great idea."

We all cross the street, Kamea and Evan talking about Sweet Infusion. Kamea still does the coffee shift in the early hours, and she's done T-shirts for Rian and Jax. Kamea's even done shirts for Evan and Seth's moms' bagel store that say, "Bagel plus Schmear Equals Best Friends." She's doing well. Pretty soon she'll be buying me things.

The detective job is awesome, although I miss Patrice. Her artificial insemination worked and though it's early she's opted for desk duty until the baby pops out just to be on the safe side. I couldn't be happier for her. Finally, after all these years, everything is fitting together and I'm not looking for anything to drop.

We walk into Ink Envy. Frankie is behind the counter, her phone out in front of her. Dylan's in the back, tattooing someone presumably, and Rian is up front with Blanca and Ethan. Sierra went to Sandsal with Adrian.

"Who wants one?" Jax swings a shirt around like a lasso.

FRANKIE ROLLS HER EYES. "I don't want anything from you."

"Oh, come on. Sit in my chair and you get one of these for free." He points at his T-shirt.

Seth is giddy with anticipation. I groan and shake my head.

Frankie's eyes narrow as she reads. "Fucking hell, I'm quitting if you hand out those damn things."

Surprisingly, she doesn't say much else. Usually she's ready to take him by the jugular.

"Frankie." My mom heads over to her. "Jolie left this letter for Santa with me on Thanksgiving at the shelter." She hands her Jolie's letter to Santa.

"Thanks so much. She told me she wrote Santa and gave it to Knox's mommy because she knows Santa, but she wouldn't tell me what she wrote. She refused to write another letter because she said he knows what she wants."

We all laugh, and Frankie opens the envelope, pulling out

the letter with a drawing. She reads it, then narrows her eyes and reads it again, losing some of her color.

"You have to be shitting me?" Frankie says, dropping it on the table.

"What? Something expensive? I'll get it for her," Jax says, picking up the letter. He's sure got a soft spot for that kid. He reads the letter and drops it as though it's on fire.

His gaze falls to Frankie, and she cocks her jaw and nods.

"What's so bad?" My mom picks it up and reads it. "Ah, this is so cute." We all step forward as my mom reads to us, "'I want Jax to be my daddy and if he can't be my daddy, I want a puppy.'"

Jax walks away without saying a word, silently tucking his container under his station.

"That's so sweet." My mom looks at Frankie.

Frankie feigns a smile, but we all know, between Jax's need to make sure Jolie has a father figure in her life and also to be her fairy godfather—making every wish come true with the flick of his tattoo gun—Frankie and Jax might just go head-to-head this holiday season.

The End

COCKAMAMIE UNICORN RAMBLINGS

Do you think we'll ever learn not to write ourselves into a corner? We hope not because most times we get such better storylines figuring our way out. We're sure some of you are surprised it wasn't Leilani that Knox ended up with. And I'm sure your question is why did you tease their relationship through three books then?

Well, truth is, it was supposed to be Knox and Leilani. We wanted to tease that second chance relationship by allowing you to see them together first. But once we got down to truly plotting out their entire story which we do right before we write, it was clear there was no conflict. If Knox loved her, there was no reason if Leilani returned for a second chance that they wouldn't just get back together. Plus, and maybe this was us, Leilani didn't come off too well the few times she was on the page. Quite simply, we didn't *want* to put him and Leilani together. She just wasn't the one for him.

So, we decided Knox needed a new woman. Someone he should've picked from the get-go. Someone who complimented his desire for a real relationship. We almost made Kamea Leilani's sister but thought that's just against sister code and couldn't do it. So, she's just her friend, but not close enough that it mattered. Anyway, we hope you enjoyed the twist that Knox's love life took with the introduction of Kamea.

Fun fact: There is a spy bar that was taken as inspiration for the one in this book in Milwaukee Wisconsin. Look it up and give it a try.

Once again, thank you to our tremendous team!

Danielle Sanchez and the entire Wildfire Marketing Solutions team.

Cassie from Joy Editing for line edits.

Ellie from My Brother's Editor for line edits.

Shawna from Behind the Writer for proofreading.

Hang Le for the cover and branding for the entire series.

Wander Aguiar for the amazing photo of Seth and Evan.

Bloggers who consistently carve out time to read, review and/or promote us.

Piper Rayne Unicorns who shout from the rooftops about our new releases and love our characters like we do.

Readers who took a chance on our book with so many choices out there.

We're sure some of you are waiting for Jax. We know once he came on page for us, we fell in love with him. He just has that special vibe and mix that with Frankie and Jolie and we can't wait to see what transpires!

XO,

Piper & Rayne

ABOUT PIPER & RAYNE

Piper Rayne, or Piper and Rayne, whichever you prefer because we're not one author, we're two. Yep, you get two USA Today Bestselling authors for the price of one. Our goal is to bring you romance stories that have "Heartwarming Humor With a Side of Sizzle" (okay...you caught us, that's our tagline). A little about us... We both have kindle's full of one-clickable books. We're both married to husbands who drive us to drink. We're both chauffeurs to our kids. Most of all, we love hot heroes and quirky heroines that make us laugh, and we hope you do, too.

The Single Dad's Club

Real Deal

Dirty Talker

Sexy Beast

Hollywood Hearts

Mister Mom

Animal Attraction

Domestic Bliss

Bedroom Games

Cold as Ice

On Thin Ice

Break the Ice

Box Set

Charity Case

Manic Monday

Afternoon Delight

Happy Hour

Blue Collar Brothers

Flirting with Fire

Crushing on the Cop

Engaged to the EMT

White Collar Brothers

Sexy Filthy Boss

Dirty Flirty Enemy

Wild Steamy Hook-up

www.ingramcontent.com/pod-product-compliance
Lightning Source LLC
Chambersburg PA
CBHW061247310726
48971CB00007B/2252